The Calling of
Elizabeth Courtland

Also by Colleen L. Reece
in Large Print:

Angel of the North
Ballad for Nurse Lark
A Girl Called Cricket
The Hills of Hope
Legacy of Silver
Mysterious Monday
Nurse Autumn's Secret Love
Nurse Camilla's Love
Thursday Trials
Trouble on Tuesday
Wednesday Witness
Friday Flight

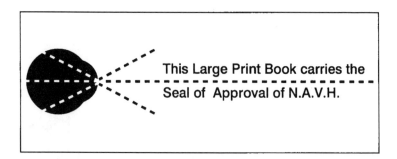

This Large Print Book carries the
Seal of Approval of N.A.V.H.

The Calling of
Elizabeth Courtland

Colleen L. Reece

Mishawaka-Penn-Harris
Public Library
Mishawaka, Indiana

Thorndike Press • Waterville, Maine

Published in 2002 by arrangement with Colleen L. Reece.

Thorndike Press Large Print Christian Romance Series.

The tree indicium is a trademark of Thorndike Press.

The text of this Large Print edition is unabridged.
Other aspects of the book may vary from the original edition.

Set in 16 pt. Plantin by Myrna S. Raven.

Printed in the United States on permanent paper.

Library of Congress Cataloging-in-Publication Data

Reece, Colleen L.
    The calling of Elizabeth Courtland / by Colleen L. Reece.
      p. cm.
    ISBN 0-7862-4087-3 (lg. print : hc : alk. paper)
    1. Children of the rich — Fiction. 2. Clergy — Fiction.
    3. Large type books. I. Title.
    PS3568.E3646 C3 2002
    813′.54—dc21   2001056372

The Calling of
Elizabeth Courtland

1

"Miss Betty, your mama says for you to come down right now!" The freckled face of the serving maid in neat gray uniform looked worried. "The carriages are coming, and Mr. Prescott's glarin' at his watch and watchin' the stairs. All the people are —" she broke off sharply. "Miss Betty, whatever is the matter?"

Elizabeth Courtland whirled from the dressing table. Her white skirts billowing about her made her look like some heavenly creature. "Abbie, have you ever been in love?"

The maid's eyes reflected her shock. "In love! Me?"

"Yes, you."

"Of course not, Miss Betty. Who'd look at the likes of me?"

Elizabeth cocked her head to one side. "Oh, I don't know. You are well put together and have shiny hair and blue eyes. A man could do worse."

Abbie just stared, then roused herself. "You'd better come. All those folks waitin' for your engagement to be announced. Your papa's goin' to be up here after you if you don't get downstairs."

"Let them wait!" The imperious head crowned with sweeping dark hair was in sharp contrast to the creamy white shoulders and snowy lace dress. "It's *my* engagement party, isn't it? I'll go down if and when I feel like it. I may not go at all."

"*Miss Betty!*"

"What's wrong, Abbie? Shocked because I'm in no hurry? Why should I be? I've been practically engaged ever since I was born." She waved a haughty hand toward the newspaper clipping on the dressing table, mocking its contents.

HOUSES OF COURTLAND AND WETHERELL TO BE JOINED
In the most lavish ball of its kind
ever to be held in Grand Rapids
Miss Elizabeth Courtland's
engagement will be announced to
Mr. Prescott Wetherell.

She dropped to the bed, appraising the Wetherell's best guest room. "Hah! What choice did *I* ever have in the matter?"

Concern for her mistress replaced Abbie's anxiety over getting her downstairs. "But Mr. Prescott just about worships you, Miss Betty! He'll give you everything you want and let you do just as you please. He's even letting me go with you to your new home just because I've always been your maid. Aren't you happy?"

At the risk of crushing her gown, Elizabeth sprang from the bed defiantly. "Why should I be? Prescott is — Prescott. As for having my own way, haven't I always?" She did not wait for a reply. "Too bad I didn't have a passel of brothers and sisters to look after. I've never had anything but my own way."

"You'll have children of your own to look after."

"Children? You must be out of your mind. Having children ruins your figure and makes you unfit for dancing."

"Yes, ma'am. But children have a way of comin' when you're married."

"Then I just won't get married!"

"Miss Betty!"

"I mean it, Abbie. I won't be tied down with children, even if nurses do look after them. It's bad enough marrying Prescott, who's dull as dishwater, but at least we can travel. He says he'll take me anywhere I want to go."

Abbie's freckles stood out at her own daring as she asked, "Miss Betty, don't you love Mr. Prescott?"

"Love Prescott Wetherell?" There was honest surprise in Elizabeth's voice. "Why should I? We've grown up together, and I'm fond of him. He's the most suitable match. Why should he want more than that?" She turned back to Abbie. "What do you know about it, anyway? You said you'd never been in love."

Abbie's face was sober. "Before my mother died she taught me never to marry a man I didn't love with all my heart. She said it was a sin to marry without love."

"Sin!" Betty broke into peals of laughter. "The only sin in this world is not doing as you please."

"Elizabeth, your guests are waiting." Mrs. Courtland's icy voice from the doorway broke into the conversation. "Abbie, I told you to send her down. Why we should have to have this engagement ball here instead of in our own home, I'll never know."

Betty chose to ignore the oft-heard complaint. "You know Prescott's mother." She linked her arm in her own mother's. "Why bother? If I'm to marry Prescott Wetherell, why not just elope?"

"That's enough from you, Elizabeth. I must say I'll be glad when you're married and safe. I'm tired of your odd remarks and wild ways. The gossip columns refer to you as 'Madcap Betty.' That's all a nice girl needs — to get herself tagged as wild. It's fortunate Prescott is so understanding."

Halfway to the top of the stairs, Abbie close behind, Betty stopped. "Mother." There was an unaccustomed tremor in her voice. "Did you love Papa when you were married? Before the ceremony, I mean?"

"Elizabeth!" Her well-padded mother drew back in horror. "What a thing to ask! No nice girl ever loves the man she marries before the wedding. Love comes afterward. It would not be dignified to have such feelings until you were married. Only a wanton would admit to it, and as for discussing —" Her voice trailed off in suggestive cadence, matching perfectly her raised eyebrows.

"That's funny. Some people think it's a sin to marry without love."

Betty cast a mischievous eye toward the frightened Abbie, but her mother cut her off. "We won't discuss it further."

"Here she comes!" A hundred pair of eyes turned toward the curving staircase into the ballroom. In a moment Betty forgot her rebellion. A tiny pulse beat in her throat. All those faces upturned, admiring her! Carefully she descended, walking as she had been taught, tiny steps in her silver slippers, swishing her train behind her in an aura of beauty.

There were Mr. and Mrs. Wetherell, dour and grim, determined to show the world that no Courtland would get ahead of them, even if she was marrying their son. There were the Ashleys and the Beaumonts and the Fosters and all the other cream of Grand Rapids society. At last her eyes singled out Prescott. After her talk with Abbie, Betty had secretly hoped he would suddenly become devastatingly handsome, mysterious, exciting. She bit her lip. He was the same Prescott she had always known — sandy haired, good-natured, smiling at her slow progress.

Betty's eyes widened. *Who is the stranger standing next to Prescott?* His hair was as dark as her own. Was that a challenge in the laughing dark eyes behind the admiration she could see from the light of a hundred candles and gas lamps? A stain of color covered her cheeks. How exciting! A new man — and evidently unattached. No belle with carefully curled hair stood next to him. What fun!

Betty came to earth with a thud. What good did it do for that handsome stranger to appear? It was her party, her engagement party.

So what? The imp of mischief that had earned her the nickname "Madcap Betty" snapped its leash. She was not married yet. Another spurt of color highlighted her already beautiful face. The stranger was too choice a prize to let slip away to some other girl.

"Elizabeth, my dear." Prescott stepped to the foot of the staircase and offered his arm. A spontaneous burst of applause interrupted her surveillance of the visitor. Bother! Why did all those people have to be there?

"May I present my good friend Daniel Spencer?" Prescott smiled at the stranger. "Dan, my fiancee, Miss Elizabeth Courtland."

Why did she feel like this? Betty's hand was swallowed in the strong grip of the stranger's. Was it mockery in the dark eyes as he murmured, "Miss Courtland"?

"Mr. Spencer." How ridiculous! Following all the courteous formalities when she longed to ask who he was and where he came from. Suddenly Betty wanted to know everything there was to know about this disturbing man. Her plans were thwarted by the arrival of her mother.

"Really, Elizabeth, Prescott! You are holding up the receiving line." Her glance set Daniel Spencer down as totally insignificant. "Come."

13

"My apologies, Mrs. Courtland." Prescott turned Betty around, but not before she caught the amused glance that Daniel Spencer gave them. Her blood boiled. He *was* laughing at her!

"Elizabeth." Her mother's whisper recalled her to the present. "Will you stop gaping at that man and stand here where you belong? Your father and I have gone to a great deal of expense to launch you as Prescott's bride. You might at least act as if you are enjoying it instead of acting like an open-mouthed fool, staring as if you had never seen a minister before!"

"Minister!" Betty stopped in mid-stride. "Mr. Spencer is a minister?"

Prescott's eyes twinkled. "Oh, yes. He's just ready to leave for the far West. He has quite an interesting story. I hope you can hear it before he goes."

Something inside Betty froze. A minister. How could a man like that be a minister? Weren't they all dreadfully self-righteous and old? Or in poor health? She stole another glance at Daniel Spencer. He was bronze — in sharp contrast to Prescott and the other men in the room. She caught his fleeting smile as he saw her looking his way. How dare he look like that? Impetuously, denying the answering thrill in her heart, she turned to Prescott with her most charming smile. Let Daniel Spencer see she had no interest in him!

Only once did Betty drop her assumed gaiety to casually ask, "What is a minister doing at a ball? I thought they were all too goody-goody to come to an event like this."

Prescott was too well-bred to show surprise at her question. "We met at college and became good friends. He said balls weren't in his line, but I insisted that he meet you. He finally gave in and came."

"How soon did you say he was leaving?"

"In a few weeks."

Someone came up, interrupting their conversation, but Betty pondered. So Daniel Spencer would be in Grand Rapids for a few weeks. Could she see him? She would like to make him fall in love with her, then turn him down hard as punishment for laughing at her.

Why did he seem to have the power to make her feel like a giddy butterfly? Was it his profession? He probably disapproved of her and all her friends. It was remarkable he did not stand up and tell them they were all sinners the way that uncle of Lydia Beaumont had done at her ball. Of course he was hurried out, but it had been terribly embarrassing. Yet she saw no accusation in the

15

dark eyes following her as she danced and flirted, only that maddening amusement.

In the midst of the ball Betty suddenly wished it was over. Why wear herself out pretending to have a good time when she was not enjoying herself at all? What was wrong with her, anyway? Was it the prospect of spending the rest of her life with Prescott Wetherell? Yet she had always known it was to be. Why should it bother her now, unless it was because the engagement party made it seem so final.

Worst of all, why did Abbie's freckled face and solemn words, "a sin to marry without love," float between Betty and her partners? She cast a scornful glance to the corner where Daniel Spencer was evidently telling a story to a group who had gathered around him. He had not danced, but then he would not, being a minister. Would he think it was a sin to marry without love? Probably. What did he know of love?

Betty was not prepared for the sharp pain that threatened to smother her and caused her partner to exclaim, "Are you all right, Miss Courtland?"

She wrenched her thoughts back to him. "Quite all right, Mr. Foster. I often catch my breath like that." Her dark eyes dared him to defy her unusual statement. Tired of him, tired of the ball, she dropped her eyelashes to make dark crescents on her flushed cheeks. "I think I'd like to sit down for a moment." She paused and calculated distance. "Perhaps over there?" She indicated a settee close enough to hear Daniel Spencer, yet far enough away so she would not rouse his suspicions, but before they could reach their chosen destination a fanfair of trumpets sounded. Prescott walked toward her.

For one moment of sheer panic Elizabeth Courtland considered fleeing through the open window into the garden, refusing to have her engagement announced. Another glance into the cool, dark eyes of the unexpected guest firmed her control. She took Prescott's arm, walked to the small dais, and mounted. Her mother beamed. Her father harrumphed and then said, "I am happy to announce the official engagement of my daughter Elizabeth to Prescott Wetherell. I present to you the bridal couple."

Betty could feel chains dropping over her, nailing her to the floor. Yet even as they dropped, she rebelled. She would not be parceled off to Prescott Wetherell before ever having really lived. So what if she had turned twenty and nice girls were married long before then? That did not mean *she* had to be.

She opened her mouth to deny the engagement — and saw Prescott looking down at her, gentle, smiling. She slowly closed her mouth. She could not hurt and humiliate him there in his own home. She would wait and tell him when he drove her to the Courtland mansion when the ball was over. Yet guilt sent red flags of color into her otherwise startlingly white face as she bowed her head and accepted the storm of congratulations following the announcement.

"Elizabeth." Prescott hurried to her side when she came down in her long evening wrap. "Mother has had a spell and needs me. I won't be able to drive you home."

Betty's heart sank. That meant another day at least before she could tell him she had changed her mind about marrying him. "I can go with Mama and Papa."

Prescott looked worried. "They've already gone."

"Allow me." Both turned to meet Daniel Spencer's steady gaze. "I will be happy to drive Miss Courtland home."

Betty's heart leaped wildly, but she managed to protest, "Really, Mr. Spencer, that won't be necessary. I am sure Prescott can get away long enough to drive me to my home."

"It's no trouble, Miss Courtland.

Prescott, your mother is calling." The inflexible mouth settled the issue.

"Thanks, Dan. Take good care of her; she's precious cargo." Prescott gripped Betty's hands, then ran lightly up the stairs.

Betty did not speak as Daniel Spencer led her to a covered carriage and tucked her inside. Swinging easily into place he took the reins. "Which way?"

"Left." Before Betty could hold them back, hot words burst out. "You don't approve of me, do you?"

"Really, Miss Courtland. I hardly know you."

The same amusement she had seen in his eyes all evening colored his voice and infuriated her. In her best Courtland manner she accused haughtily, "I know you don't. I could see it all evening. Just why don't you like me?" He started to reply, but she forestalled him. "Remember, you are a minister. You need not lie to be polite."

"I never lie, Miss Courtland." His voice was colder than the icy breath of Lake Michigan when she had visited it once in winter. "You are a beautiful girl. You are also thoroughly spoiled — and you do not love Prescott Wetherell in the way you should in order to be his wife."

"Nice girls learn to love their husbands

after marriage, Mr. Spencer," she told him primly.

"Rubbish!" She could see his hands tighten on the reins as he turned slightly toward her in the early morning dimness. "It is a crime to marry without love."

"You and Abbie!"

"Abbie?"

"My maid. She seems to be quite an authority on love. She told me much the same thing before I came down tonight." Betty bit her lip. Why had she revealed Abbie's words to this man?

"She is a wise maid. Too bad you didn't listen better."

"What right do you have to speak to me like this, Mr. Spencer?"

"The right of a man called by God to teach foolish children something of His will in their lives."

"You consider me a child?" The ominous note in her voice should have warned him.

It did not even slow him down. "Certainly. A petted child who is of no earthly use except to look pretty. Tell me, Miss Courtland, can you bake a loaf of bread such as your cook bakes? Can you make a dress such as your seamstress makes? Can you even make a bed, or dry a dish, or keep your clothing in order, as I'm sure your little maid Abbie now does? If something happened that you had to provide for yourself and keep from starving — could you do it?"

"You are impertinent, sir!"

He suddenly sounded weary. "No, I am realistic. I see you girls who have not been given a chance to learn anything important in life and —"

"*Important!* I can ride and dance and play the piano and —"

"And flirt and starve to death if your life depended on your own skills!"

"No one has ever talked to me like this!"

"Then isn't it time someone did? I'll be gone in a few weeks. Shall I tell you what it will be like where I am going?" He did not wait for her answer — probably would not have heard if she had spoken it, Betty realized.

"I am going to a town out West called Pioneer. It is carved from the heart of a great forest by men who are as rugged as the trees they cut to make homes for their families. There are seven saloons. There is one small grocery store. There is a railroad into town and enough children for a one-room school. Could you teach eight grades in one room, Miss Courtland, as the brave little teacher does? Could you hoe corn and plant beans and wash your own clothing on a scrub

21

board with water you had hauled from a creek?"

"I could if I had to. I never will have to."

"Ah, yes." Betty caught the mirth in his voice. "If you had to. I doubt it, Miss Courtland. Perhaps I shouldn't blame you too much. I am sure your parents have encouraged you to fritter away your life and eventually marry Prescott Wetherell and raise daughters just as useless as yourself. Well, let me tell you this, Miss Elizabeth Courtland. You have never lived. You will never live or love until you find the place in this world God created for you to fill, and then fill it with all your strength."

Betty could hardly keep from striking him. "And you think that place is *not* as Prescott Wetherell's wife! Could it be that you are simply jealous, Mr. Spencer? Jealous of Prescott and his wealth and position?" She warmed to her subject, hands clenched in her lap. "If you could trade places with Prescott, wouldn't you do so — and gladly?"

"Never!" The vehement word rang in the still night.

He reined in the horses and turned to her. "Nothing on earth could induce me to live the indolent life you and your friends live — even Prescott. I had hopes for him in college. He would have made a brilliant lawyer.

It was all he ever wanted to do."

Betty gasped.

"You didn't know that, did you, Miss Courtland? There are a lot of things you don't know about Prescott. He gave up his plans because his selfish, petted mother, who once was just like you, demanded he come home and be with her during her 'spells.' The only thing wrong with Prescott Wetherell's mother is her temper. If she had to fend for herself and would let her son be a man, she would find those 'spells' strangely absent."

"Why didn't Prescott break free, if he wanted it so badly?" There were disbelief and shock in her voice.

"Why don't you break free of the useless life you lead?"

"I, sir, am a lady." She drew herself up, angry at herself for listening to him for so long.

Daniel started the horses once more. His voice was colorless, his impassioned words cooled to ice. "That may be, Miss Courtland, but I pray the day will come when God will allow you to forget the lady part and become a real woman."

Betty was stung more than ever before in her life, shaken by his words. "I suppose you could teach me to be a real woman."

"I could." His jawline was hard. "But frankly, I don't want the job. When I find a wife it will be one who can be a helpmate and companion, not someone to be waited on and pampered. Why, you couldn't even be the fit mother of a child, Miss Courtland."

"Sir!"

"If I shock you it is because I mean to do just that. Name one qualification you have for motherhood, for the daring challenge of raising a human being to be more than you yourself are." He broke off. "Is this your home?"

Betty nodded wordlessly, unable to get anything past the gigantic mound in her throat. Finally she said, "If you believed me so worthless, why did you come to the ball to meet me?"

He helped her from the carriage and stood facing her in the pale light. "I came because I was curious. Curious about a society girl with enough spirit to be called 'Madcap Betty.' Perhaps I thought she would be more than the typical belle — with warmth and humor and love for Prescott."

"*And?*" The single word nearly choked her.

"I found a spoiled child. One who will never make Prescott happy or be happy herself." His words were grave, almost sad.

Betty struggled with tears as the mansion door opened; the impassive butler stared woodenly ahead. Every invective she could dredge up to hurt this man who had been judge and jury, tried and condemned her, damming up behind her frozen lips.

"Good night, Miss Courtland. No, good morning."

A tip of that hat, a spring to the carriage, and he was gone, leaving a shaken Betty Courtland peering after him into the dawn of a new and unwelcome day.

2

"How dare he?" Betty paced the floor of her own room, white skirts trailing. She had swept up the staircase so like the one in the Wetherell mansion she had descended in triumph earlier that evening but with such a difference. So she was a spoiled child? She would show him. But how?

For hours she walked, heedless of servants arising, a new day in full swing. Her anger grew, at herself as well as at Daniel Spencer. How could she have allowed him to speak so, condemning her and others like her? Why should she care what he thought — the country dolt? He would go to his precious town of Pioneer and she would never have to hear of him again.

But before he goes, I will repay him. I will entrap him, make him fall in love with me, then throw in his face how different we are by parroting his exact words to me! An unpleasant smile marred the classic features, turned the blue eyes almost to black. She dropped to the dressing table bench and stared at her misty reflection.

Suppose — suppose I should marry him, then

run off and leave him! Her face glowed at the plan. She sprang to her feet and ran to the window, throwing wide the curtains. "I'll do it! I'll even marry him — then have the time of my life when I tell him I'm getting a divorce! A minister with a divorce. That should ruin him forever!"

A perplexed frown crossed her face. "I wonder where I should begin?" She paced the carpeted floor again. "Perhaps I could play the part of a penitent — pretend I really took to heart what he said. I wonder if I could learn to cook?" She shuddered. "Horrors!" Yet a moment later her chin was set. "I'll do it if I have to. I'll get even with Daniel Spencer if it's the last thing I do."

Betty slumped to a big chair, suddenly drained. The night of dancing followed by Daniel's indictment and her determination had left her exhausted. But there was no time to waste in sleeping. He would only be in Grand Rapids a little while. She must not waste any of that time.

Imperiously she rang her bell to summon Abbie. The maid responded with wide eyes. "Miss Betty, you're still in your ball gown. Didn't you go to bed?"

"Never mind that. Get me some breakfast up here on a tray. Then get out my driving clothes. I have a call to make."

"At nine o'clock in the morning?" Abbie's voice oozed disapproval.

"Oh, bother, Abbie. Do as I say! I'm going to see how Mrs. Wetherell is after her spell last night." For one moment the eyes of the two girls met in perfect understanding. Mrs. Wetherell's "spells" were known to both of them — an excuse to keep Prescott close at hand.

"Yes, ma'am."

In an incredibly short time Abbie was back. Betty stuffed a little breakfast in her mouth, dressing as she ate. Through a mouthful she mumbled, "Have Sam bring the small carriage around with Beauty. I'll drive myself."

"Miss Betty, your mama ain't goin' to like it."

"So?" Again her level glance quieted Abbie. She even laughed and waved good-bye to the still disapproving figure as she lifted the reins and drove down the avenue she had traveled the night before in company with Daniel Spencer. The clear morning and fresh air whipped color into her face. She had taken the first step. Now if things would only work out as she hoped at the Wetherells.

They did. The Wetherell butler was quite surprised to see Miss Courtland at such an early hour, especially after a ball. "Why, why, Miz Wetherell isn't up. I'll get Mr. Prescott." He scuttled away, nearly upsetting a vase of flowers in his hurry, muttering to himself, "Callers. Nine o'clock in the morning. That woman must be up to something!"

"Betty, my dear," Prescott's face was alight with surprise.

"I just came to see how your mother is."

Prescott's smile faded. "Not so well. She seems to have overtaxed her strength at our engagement ball. She plans to spend the day in bed." He looked at Betty apologetically. "I'm afraid I'll have to stay around. She gets so upset if she calls and I'm not here."

Without thinking Betty asked, "Prescott, is that why you gave up the study of law?"

He froze in place. It was a long moment before he answered. "Yes, Elizabeth. She was so against it —"

Betty's anger at Mrs. Wetherell mixed with contempt for Prescott. "I think you should do what you feel is right."

"It's all right." He managed a crooked smile. "Just knowing we'll be married will make up for it." His laugh was shaky. "Who wants to spend all their time in a stuffy court, anyway?"

Now was the time to tell him she was not

planning to marry him. Betty could not do it. Instead she said, "I'd hoped you would be free to drive in the country with me. I've been promising our old cook to stop by for weeks, and today's such a beautiful day. Mama would have fits if I went by myself." She managed just the right amount of wistfulness.

"I'm sorry, Betty," he took both her hands. "I just can't." His face brightened. "Say, why can't Dan go with you? He's top company. Didn't you get along capitally with him last night on the way home?" Carried away by his own enthusiasm Prescott rang for the butler. "Ask Mr. Dan to come in here, will you please?"

Betty felt like a hypocrite as she protested, "Oh, don't bother, Prescott. I'm sure Mr. Spencer has other plans. I can put off going until another day."

"Don't be silly. He'll be delighted to go. Not much fun for him hanging around here."

"Good morning, Prescott, Miss Courtland." There was nothing in Daniel Spencer's voice to show he had ever said anything more to Miss Courtland than a formal hello. Betty's eyes took in every detail. He was even more striking in worn clothing than he had been in formal garb.

There was something outdoorsy in the careless way his shirt was open at the neck.

"Elizabeth had plans to pay a visit to her old cook out in the country today, and I can't go," Prescott explained. "I suggested you would accompany her."

"Delighted, of course." His eyes bored into Betty. Did he wonder why Betty would have any interest in a cook? Betty's ruse became reality. She *would* visit the cook.

"I tried to tell Prescott the visit could wait." She lifted innocent eyes toward Daniel Spencer, knowing full well how she looked with the shaft of sunlight streaming through the draperies to highlight her. "He thought you might enjoy seeing some of our countryside while you were here, and as he isn't free —" she lifted one shoulder daintily.

She was rewarded by a flash of humor mixed with admiration. "I am sure I will enjoy seeing — the countryside."

"Very well." She turned back to Prescott to hide her confusion. Somehow she had not fooled Daniel Spencer at all. It would take all the skill she had to convince him of her sincerity. "Good-bye, Prescott." She gazed up at him fondly, still aware of Dan's eyes on her. "Give your mother my sympathy."

Daniel Spencer did not speak until they were in the light carriage and well on their way out of the city. "Miss Courtland, you didn't really appear on the Wetherell doorstep at nine in the morning to see how Mrs. Wetherell was, did you?"

Betty decided to drop her pose, at least for the time being. "No, Mr. Spencer, I came to see if I could inveigle you into a drive with me." She caught his involuntary slowing of the horses and added rapidly, "I wanted to tell you I spent several hours after you left taking inventory of myself. You were right. I really have not been good for anything important in life until now." A passing breeze stirred one long lock of raven hair. "I also wanted to ask you —" The tremble in her voice was real. "Do you think I could change? Could I become the woman you said God wanted me to be?" She felt, rather than saw, his suspicious glance and hurried on. "I didn't sleep at all. I felt I had to see you."

"I see, Miss Courtland." He hesitated. "Am I to understand then that the casual words of a stranger could so affect you?"

"Casual!" Betty repeated. "You accused, tried, and convicted me all in the space of minutes."

"I know." His grasp of the reins tightened.

"I believe I was very rude. I had no right to come into your life and speak so."

Betty leaned forward, eyes on the road they traveled. "I am glad you came into my life, Mr. Spencer. You will never know just what it meant to me." It was the truth, she knew. Under lowered lashes she saw him turn toward her and played her trump card. "You said God had a plan for every person's life. How do I find what it is in my life?"

Just ahead and off the road stood a big oak. Toward it Daniel guided Beauty until she stood quietly beneath the leafy branches. "Miss Courtland, if you are sincere, if you desire to change your life, there is no reason you cannot do so. God stands ready to accept you. When you take the first steps toward Him, He does the rest in receiving you."

Betty shivered in spite of herself. What was she getting herself into? She took refuge in a question. "Mr. Spencer, tell me. How did a man such as you, who went to college with Prescott, decide to become a minister?"

"It's a long story." Yet he looked at her wistfully.

"We have the whole day." Her smile encouraged him to spring from the carriage and throw a blanket on the ground under the big tree. Helping her down, he stood before her, his face lifted to the sky. Was he *praying?* What if he were praying for *her?* The next moment he dropped to the blanket beside her.

"Miss Courtland, from the time I was small I knew someday God would ask me to serve Him." His solemn voice sent shivers up Betty's spine.

"My father was a minister. We always had enough to eat and wear but never any luxuries. Yet I remember the faces of those who loved him. Wherever we were sent, he left a trail of hope. He worked with doctors, often bringing comfort when medicine failed. It was my father who introduced me to Jesus Christ." Betty knew she had been forgotten, and a pang of envy filled her. What a different childhood he had known! If only her family had been close like that.

"I must have been about seven when he started taking me with him on some of his calls. He had fought in the Civil War, and when he came home he wanted no more fighting. He would spend the rest of his life fighting a different battle.

"I will never forget the day a man he had worked with to help find a better life reverted to his old ways and took his own life. My father's brow was furrowed. Young as I

34

was, I realized what a blow it had been. I asked, 'Father, isn't it like losing a battle?' He always compared the fight for men's souls to the fight for men's freedom.

"He looked at me for a full minute before he said, 'Son, losing the battle isn't so important. Winning the war is.' I believe at that moment I knew I was to follow in my father's footsteps. He insisted that I get schooling, be better prepared to meet some of the modern questions and indifference than he had been. I finished college and was assigned to a small church in Kansas. Then my real call came — to build my own church for God in a place that desperately needs it."

Betty found moisture on her hands. Had it slid from brimming eyes at the touching story? "Why didn't you take a real church, one in a huge city where there are hundreds of people who need you?" Neither noticed the absence of hostility between them.

"I considered it. I even had an opportunity for a church right here in Grand Rapids." He named a large church she knew well.

"Daniel." The unaccustomed name felt strange on her lips. "Could you still have that church?"

"Yes. But I will not take it."

"Why not?" Hot color stung her cheeks.

"Don't you think there are people here in Grand Rapids who could benefit by what you have to offer? You could have money and prestige and make a name for yourself."

"The name I make must be for my God, not for myself."

Betty was silenced. Yet her agile mind seized on another facet. "You have education. You could reach the cultured. What need do people such as those in your town of Pioneer have for such education? Does your God want all your training wasted?"

"The loggers in Pioneer need God's message as well as the elite in Grand Rapids."

"But someone else could go there! Someone who isn't so well-prepared, someone who couldn't handle the church here. Why, with your friendship with Prescott Wetherell, all the best people would attend your church. You could reach ten or a hundred times as many people as will ever respond in that dump out West."

"The gospel of Jesus Christ is for all, Miss Courtland. I do not need the Wetherell backing in order to present my Lord."

Betty stared. "Then you really will throw away a chance like that, just because of your pride in what you believe? Aren't you being self-righteous?"

She was prepared for anything except

what happened. Daniel Spencer laughed until the leaves above them shook. "Self-righteous! My dear Miss Courtland, have you any idea what a snob you really are?" He was off again, his gales of laughter sweeping through the clear morning air.

"Really!" Betty jumped to her feet but tripped over the hem of her long skirt. He caught her, for one moment holding her while she regained her footing. The touch of his strong hands unnerved her. Angrily she jerked free. How could she respond to such a boor?

"You are a fanatic, Mr. Spencer. No one in his right mind would make the choice you are making. And while we are on the subject, I am not your dear Miss Courtland. I belong to Prescott Wetherell."

"Do you, Miss Courtland?" There was a disturbing gleam in his dark eyes. "I think not. You belong to only one."

"Who? Not you, I dare say," she flouted him, a sarcastic smile touching her lips. "You wouldn't be crazy enough to believe that."

"Not at all. You could never belong to me."

In spite of her fury something inside hurt at his words. "Then just whom are you referring to?"

"God."

"God! *I?* I am not even sure a God exists. How could I belong to Him?" She saw she had overplayed her role. Where had the assurance that she could fake an interest and wind him around her finger gone? "I mean," she added hastily, "I've never known anyone who could show me there really was a God. Perhaps you could do that?"

"I wish I could!" His vehemence startled her. "I wish I could show you how precious you are to that God you say may not exist. You think it is chance you were born in beauty and luxury? No. It is part of God's plan, as surely as those trees and flowers are part of it." He waved across open fields to clumps of trees surrounded with blossoms. "How can you look at all that beauty and not see God's hand!"

"Why, it's always been there," she faltered, unsure of herself against his strength. "Ever since I can remember, it's always been there."

"And before your remembrance? Before your parents and their parents? What then?"

Betty put her head in her hands. "It tires me to think of it. Why not just have a good time in life? Why spend it by thinking deep and solemn thoughts? Your God makes long faces. I've seen them, the holier-than-thous who sneer at me when I ride by. Even if there is a God, what would I have to do with Him?"

"Miss Courtland, will you sit down again, please? I think you might like to hear a story about a great woman."

Betty eyed him distrustfully, then re-seated herself. What woman would he speak of, some paragon he planned to marry? She pushed back a twinge at the idea and regarded him with unfriendly eyes. "Perhaps you had better make your story short, Mr. Spencer. I really do have other things to do today."

If he caught the bald contradiction from her earlier statement he ignored it. Leaning against the tree trunk, hands clasped behind his head, Daniel Spencer seemed part of the outdoor world itself. Betty resented the effect he had on her. Why should her heart pound at his nearness, the resonant note in his deep voice?

"You say you think God makes long faces. The most beautiful woman I ever knew didn't find God that way at all."

Betty drew in a sharp breath, nails biting into her clenched hands. So it was true. He would parade the virtues of some distant fiancee before her, showing by comparison how wicked and inadequate she was. She stared stonily at Beauty as he began.

"She never had much, but everywhere she went people loved her. Fretful children stilled under her hand. Old people smiled, and young people laughed when she came. Her home was open to all. There was music and fun — not balls and luncheons and teas such as you need to survive, but the joy of living. She worked twelve hours a day gardening, mending, sewing, cooking — yet found time to watch every sunset, hear every bird song, see every early spring flower. She taught others to do the same.

"Jesus Christ walked with her. Whether she sat mending stockings or was picking berries for jelly and jam, God was there. She saw Him in every cloud. Do you know why, Miss Courtland? Because first of all, she had Him in her heart. They called her 'Mrs. Minister' instead of by her name. The ministry she gave equalled, if not surpassed, what her husband was able to do. You asked me what God wanted in your life. If you could ever become half the woman Mrs. Minister was, you would be the happiest, most loved person on earth."

Mrs. Minister. In a flash Betty knew. The woman he spoke of must be his wife. But he had said *was*.

"You said *was*. Isn't she living?" The words forced themselves through her tight throat. Why did she care? Why did she, Elizabeth Courtland, hold her breath waiting for his answer?

"No. She died as she lived — gloriously. The last thing she ever said was, 'I'll be waiting for you all — with Jesus.' "

"And she changed your life, made you willing to go out to that place, Pioneer, to live in squalor and dust and crudeness?"

Daniel Spencer seemed to have moved a thousand miles away. "Yes, Miss Courtland. Because of her, I am not only willing to go — I am eager."

Betty's lips felt still. Nothing on earth could have held back the question. "She — Mrs. Minister was your wife?"

Blank dismay greeted her comment. "Of course not, Miss Courtland. I am not married. Mrs. Minister was my mother."

3

"Your *mother?*" Relief washed through Betty, leaving her furious with herself. Why should she care that Daniel Spencer's ideal was not a former wife?

"Certainly, Miss Courtland. She followed my father wherever he was sent. She could make a home of the simplest surroundings. I wish you could have known her."

"She probably wouldn't have liked me," Betty blurted. She was shocked at her own frankness. "She wouldn't have approved of me."

"She would have liked you."

But not approved. The unspoken words hung in the air between them. Betty dropped her head forward so her hair would hide the flush in her face. It was nothing to her that Daniel Spencer's ideal woman would have despised her for the way she lived. Defiantly she stood, ignoring the churning emotions inside that had been triggered by his story.

"I believe we had better go, Mr. Spencer. Thank you for the story." There was nothing in the colorless words to show the impact that same story had made on her.

"Very well, Miss Courtland." Good heavens, could the man read her mind? Stiffly she accepted his offer of help, but once in the carriage she kept silent. The day that had started so joyously was spoiled. She could not even think of a subject of conversation.

"It's very kind of you to go to all this trouble to visit your old cook." Was there disbelief in his voice? Betty controlled her feelings enough to reply, "I was always fond of her," and suddenly realized it was true. She who had treated servants as servants and nothing else, with the exception of Abbie, realized she *had* missed Emma since the cook grew too old to work for the family.

The cottage they finally reached was tiny but immaculate. Was it much like the home Daniel's mother would have created from such a building? Neatly planted flowers broke the earth on each side of a little walk. White curtains floated at the miniature windows. The whole house was not much bigger than Betty's bedroom, but there was a good smell of stew in a kettle in the fireplace.

"Why, Miss Betty," Emma's crone-like face burst into a sunburst of wrinkles. "How nice of you to come! You said you would, but I'd about given up hope." She glanced approvingly at Daniel looming in the doorway behind Betty. "And is this your young man? I heard you had become engaged."

Betty turned fiery red but was saved by Daniel's deep reply. "Sorry, I'm not the one. Prescott was busy so I took his place."

"Well, now, that's kind. Won't you sit down?" She crossed to her kettle and stirred the contents. "I was just about ready to have a wee bit of stew. You'll join me?" There was nothing in her manner to indicate any difference in station. Betty marveled. Was that what happened when one was independent of others? Mrs. Minister would have greeted guests in much the same way, Betty knew with a flash of insight. Could she herself ever — ?

"I'd love some." Betty shut off her train of thought and flashed a smile. "Mr. Spencer, no one makes stew like Emma."

"I can tell that by the smell." The look he gave the old lady endeared him to Betty. "Let me lift the kettle from the hook for you."

"Thank you, laddie." Emma ladled steaming stew into plates Betty recognized as having been discarded from her own household. There were a few chips from the edges, but they were still beautiful. What would it be like to exist on hand-me-downs? The quick glance around the cottage showed nearly all the furnishings had originally been Courtland possessions. Yet there was something in the room that was not to be found in the mansion where Betty lived. Was it — peace? She scoffed at the idea. What could this old retired cook have that she would want?

"We'll just have a word o' prayer." Emma bowed her head, and Betty stared. "Father, we thank Thee for this food and these friends. Bless both. Amen."

Betty's spoon struck the edge of her bowl as she raised it, fingers trembling. How disgusting, getting upset over an old woman's prayer! There were always prayers at the Courtland table mumbled, it was true, but a formal grace by the head of the household. Yet Emma's prayer had been almost like a petition to a friend. From under her lowered lashes Betty caught Daniel's quick glance toward her. That would be right along his line.

"Do come back, Miss Betty, and you too, sir." Their white-haired hostess waved from the doorway as they climbed into the carriage for the long trip home.

"Good-bye, Emma, and thanks." Betty

was still waving when they rounded the corner by the fence and drove out of sight.

"She's certainly a wonderful person, isn't she?"

Betty answered soberly, "Yes, she is. I felt closer to her today than all the time she worked for us." Her fingers played with her purse. "I wonder why?"

"In your home you were mistress and servant. In her home you were equals."

"Equal? Myself and a servant?" Betty could not hold back her indignation.

"I beg your pardon, Miss Courtland." Was there mockery in his careful apology? "I should not have called you equals. Your friend Emma has something you do not have, so really you are not equal at all."

"And pray tell what might that be?" Betty's jaw was set as she hurled the question at him.

"She has the joy of knowing that she is in exactly the right place in this world, the one God prepared for her."

"Why, you — you —"

Daniel laughed softly as if enjoying it. "I probably am whatever you choose to call me, but I still hold that Emma is a far wiser and happier person than you are, Miss Elizabeth 'Madcap Betty' Courtland!"

If the conversation had languished before,

46

it suffered sudden death at that moment. "I really don't care to discuss it." Icicles tinkled in Betty's retort. She folded her hands in her lap and turned her head away to hide the vexation swelling from the tip of her toes to her all-betraying eyes.

It did not daunt him. To her amazement he started whistling, of all things! How could he whistle after insulting her the way he had? Perhaps she was being too hard on him; he was just a country lout. Yet he had gone to the same college as Prescott. It was not lack of manners but poor manners that caused him to plague her.

"Will your parents be concerned over your absence?"

"Why should they? I do as I please."

"Amen to that!" His wide grin was enough to drive her insane. For one moment she considered throwing her small purse straight at his head. No, she would not give him the satisfaction of knowing how he had scored. Instead she maintained her glowering silence until they reached the edge of the city.

"Go straight to the Wetherells. Perhaps Prescott will be free to drive me home," she ordered, deliberately using the same tone she would have used to her coachman.

"Certainly not, Miss Courtland. I

couldn't allow such a thing. If Prescott was not free this morning, he will not be free now. I will drive you home and walk back."

"Walk! It is miles!"

"So it is." Behind his mild surprise lay more laughter, stinging Betty anew.

"I insist you go to the Wetherells!"

"Sorry. If you choose to drive there yourself when I have gone, that is your affair."

Was there ever such an infuriating clod? Betty counted to ten. "Very well." The cauldron of anger threatened to erupt. "If you insist on being a fool, I won't stop you."

"You couldn't anyway," he gently reminded. "You see, Miss Courtland, I am also in the habit of doing — what I think is right."

When they reached her home Abbie was on the porch, her face as disapproving in the early evening gloom as it had been that morning. "Your mama wants you right away." The ominous note in her voice raised the corners of Daniel Spencer's lips in another grin and sent a quick pang through Betty. She would be in for it; that was obvious. And for what? She had made no headway at all in her plan to entrap Daniel with her charms.

As a last-minute maneuver she abruptly did an about-face. "Mr. Spencer, I did appreciate your escorting me. I also —" She swallowed the word *enjoyed* as too much even for him to accept. "I found your stories quite enlightening. I hope you will call, perhaps tomorrow?" There! She had left the way open.

"If Prescott is not able to come and wishes me to do so, I will call." He turned back toward the carriage. "Shall I take Beauty to the stable before letting your fiance know you are safely home?" There was just the slightest shade of emphasis on *fiance*.

"Of course not," she snapped. "My man will do that." Without even a good-bye she turned haughtily and swept through the door Abbie held open. The insufferable prig, reminding her she was engaged to Prescott!

"You'd better see your mama," Abbie reminded. Betty whirled on her. "I'll see her after I've bathed and changed. I don't know why I went anyway — out in that dusty country just to see Emma. Get out my yellow gown, Abbie, and stop that chattering."

Mrs. Courtland's anger strangely rolled off Betty. She merely stared at her mother, listening to the accusations of impropriety. "Riding the whole day with a man you barely know! If Prescott couldn't take you as his affianced wife, then you knew better than to go off with that — that preacher!"

"He was perfectly proper." Betty yawned daintily, covering her mouth with her fingers.

"It doesn't matter. What will people say?"

"Who cares?" Betty's languor vanished. "I'm tired of living where it is according to what 'they say' and 'they think.' Mother, have you ever done one single thing in your life without wondering how 'they' will react?"

Mrs. Courtland snorted. "I certainly hope not! Pleasing society is the most important thing in life."

"Is it?" Betty's thoughts were upon an oak tree, blue sky, and flowers surrounding a strong man who gazed at them. "What about pleasing God?"

"God!" It was Mrs. Courtland's turn to stare. "That is positively blasphemous, Elizabeth, to speak of God in that familiar way." She rose magnificently and walked toward the door. "I suggest you do some serious thinking about what you have done this day and be ready to apologize to Prescott when you next see him." The door banged shut behind her, leaving Betty feeling again as if a prison door had closed her in.

The fresh air should have made Betty sleepy. It did not. She paced the floor as she had done the night before, memories churning. In vain she flayed herself for caring what Daniel Spencer thought. When she finally did prepare for bed and turn out her light, it was to find his face floating in the darkness. Sometime later another face seemed to join him — the face of a woman, laughing, with workworn hands. Betty knew it must be Mrs. Minister, the one who had found God not formidable but a companion.

A vague and fleeting wish crossed Betty's heart, too slight to register more than an imprint. Would Mrs. Minister really have disapproved, or would she have seen something — it was too nebulous. At last Betty slept.

Sunlight streamed through her curtains when Betty awoke. She stretched deliciously, at peace with the world — until the sharp pressure of the ring Prescott had placed on her finger brought her back to reality with a thud. She had to break her engagement — today. Daniel Spencer might be odious, but he had been right about one thing. She did not love Prescott. She had sensed it when she spoke to Abbie. It had been confirmed at the actual

51

announcing of her engagement.

Sluggishly she slid from bed, impatiently calling, "Come in," to the knock on her door. Abbie's curly head appeared. Her capable hands carried a tray. She set it on a bedside table and threw wide the drapes, letting in even more sunlight.

"Good mornin', Miss Betty." Abbie uncovered plates. "Fresh berries and cream. Hot toast. An egg, just the way you like it." She poured cream into the coffee. "Anything else?"

"Yes — no — Abbie, stop rushing off so soon. Sit down, and talk while I eat."

Abbie's eyes sparkled. It was not often her mistress requested such a thing. Usually after being up late the night before Betty was in no mood to talk with anyone, let alone her maid.

"Was Mama really upset yesterday?"

Abbie's lips turned down. "*Was she!* First she asked where you'd gone at the ungodly hour of nine. Then she waited lunch for you until the souffle fell. She finally sent Sam over to the Wetherells to find out when you'd be home. She wasn't very happy when Prescott sent word you'd gone into the country with that Mr. Spencer."

"I see."

Abbie leaned forward, confidential. "I

reckon she's afraid of what Miz Wetherell might think."

"I reckon she is," Betty mimicked, suddenly losing her appetite. Must she always be bound by convention, by what others expected? "Take it away, Abbie. I'm not hungry."

"But you've scarcely eaten a bite!"

"Take it away, I tell you. I don't want it. Then come back and help me dress."

When Abbie returned, it was with a scowl on her face. "He's here."

"Who's here? Prescott? I can't see him. I'm not ready for the day."

"Not Prescott. Him." She jerked a thumb toward the open window. Betty threw a robe over her gown and ran to the window.

"Daniel Spencer!"

"In a carriage, even. Looks like Mr. Prescott's carriage. What's he doin' here?" she demanded sourly.

"How should I know? Help me get dressed, Abbie."

"Why don't I just tell him to go away?"

"No!"

Abbie's face showed growing understanding. "So that's the way of it. You're interested in him — after all Mr. Prescott's done for you."

"Don't be ridiculous!" Betty managed a

scornful laugh. "He's Mr. Prescott's guest, a preacher. I have to be courteous to him."

"Don't much look like a preacher in that rig. Looks more like someone comin' to court."

Betty was furious. So that was what came of being friendly with servants. "It's none of your business, Abbie. Fasten my dress."

"Yes, ma'am." But Abbie's look of gloom reflected in the mirror, and Betty refused to meet it. Some of the anger from the day before had faded. All Betty could think of was that Daniel Spencer was downstairs.

"Yes?" Her voice was cool when she entered the library. He stood in front of the great fireplace, cold now. She was struck by his height, even more than when she had seen him before.

"Prescott asked me to come. His mother is feeling no better, and he said you had had plans for luncheon and a musicale that would need an escort."

Betty had completely forgotten her plans for the day. Now she hastily consulted her mental engagement book. "Oh, yes, at the Beaumonts'. It really wasn't necessary for you to come, Mr. Spencer."

"Prescott thought it was, and as his guest —" He shrugged his shoulders indifferently, setting Betty simmering again. "So

54

this is where you live."

"Obviously." She watched him survey the room, seeing it through his eyes instead of her own. The choice furniture, priceless rugs and drapes, the formal elegance of beautifully bound but little read books. Did he recognize their rarity, the first editions?

"Well?" She could not refrain from asking.

"It is tasteful, of course. Do you ever have a fire?"

"When it is chilly. I'm afraid I really don't spend much time in here." Her light laugh hung in the semi-gloom.

"I thought not."

"I suppose you prefer that one-room shack of Emma's." *He certainly has the talent for bringing out the worst in me.*

"I do." He crossed to a shelf, removed one of Scott's works, opened it. "Hm. Doesn't look as if it is used often." He replaced it and turned back to her. "I like to see books read and reread. We never had many, but they were always tattered from being loved. I used to dig out an old favorite on a rainy day. It was like a visit to a friend."

"Remarkable. But I suppose those in poverty must find some outlet for their leisure moments." Betty knew she sounded like the snob he thought she was but could not resist the dig.

"There are many kinds of poverty, Miss Courtland, not just financial. I find poverty of the mind and soul the hardest to understand."

Betty could not trust herself to speak. She swept toward the door and tossed over her shoulder, "I'll be ready to leave for the luncheon at twelve sharp. I hate to be kept waiting."

"So do I."

Betty ran across the marble floor and up the great staircase to her own room. Flushed, ruffled, she sped to the window and watched him leisurely stroll out to his carriage. Evidently he had not waited for Sam to let him out the massive front doors. She saw him stop and deliberately look over the entire estate, then caught the shrug of his shoulders as he climbed into the carriage and lifted the reins. His back was as straight as the chairs in the dining room as he drove away.

There was another argument with her mother before Betty escaped to the luncheon. It started when Mrs. Courtland marched in to see why Betty was not ready and why Prescott had sent "that man" in his place. "You're not wearing that, I hope!"

She frowned at the gauzy yellow dress. "That's the first of your trousseau frocks."

"It's mine. I'll wear it when I please."

"Elizabeth, you are a wicked, unnatural child. Take that dress off, and put on one of your old ones."

"I will not!" The fire in Betty's eyes matched that in her mother's. "I said I'd marry Prescott to please you, but I'm not married yet! I'll wear what I please, when I please, and with whom I please. And I wish you'd stop referring to Mr. Spencer as 'that man.' You know his name perfectly well. Do you also know that he's been offered the pastorate of the biggest church in Grand Rapids?"

"Well!" Mrs. Courtland's shock was complete. "I would never have suspected it. Perhaps there is more to this young man than one would suppose. I will have to cultivate his acquaintance. After all, he is a friend of Prescott's and —"

"He isn't taking the position." Betty took wicked delight in the way her mother's face fell. "He's going out West just like he'd planned and build some dinky church in some dump of a town where he'll have loggers and birds and squirrels for a congregation."

"I forbid you to go anywhere with him,

Elizabeth! If he is doing that, he must be insane!" She bustled further into the room. "Or worse, he is a fanatic. You can't be too careful about him. He may hypnotize you, and you'll be wanting to go off with him!"

"He wouldn't take me if I wanted to go." Betty regretted her thrust as soon as she made it. "That is, can you imagine me wanting to ever be a minister's wife? Heaven help the minister who married me!" She pushed past her mother toward the top of the stairs.

"But Betty, you mustn't go with this man to the luncheon. What will people say?"

"I really don't care." Betty raced downstairs in her yellow dress to where Daniel Spencer waited, chiding herself for her unreasonable excitement, but unable to still her leaping heart.

4

"You're in love with her, aren't you, Dan?" The words were infinitely sad but held no accusation.

Daniel Spencer whirled toward Prescott. He opened his lips to utter a denial, but only produced a hoarse laugh. Finally he said, "Can you imagine a match between 'Madcap Betty' and myself?"

"I not only can, I do." Prescott faced him squarely, eyes steady. "Don't try and apologize, old friend. I've known since we were children that Elizabeth did not love me the way a woman should love." His voice faltered a bit. "I hoped in time she would learn."

"She will! She has to." Daniel paced the floor of the Wetherell library. "She couldn't find a better man anywhere, or one who would cherish her the way you would do. As for me —" Suddenly strength flowed into his determined face. "I have to be honest with you, Prescott. The first time I saw Elizabeth Courtland something struck me — the way she held her head like a proud, wild thing. When I found she was to be betrothed to you something in me died before it had been fully born. As I learned to know what a selfish person she is, I rejoiced. Nothing could ever come of my first feeling."

"Yet you love her."

"Love? Or is it simply attraction for what I know I can never have?" Daniel's smile was crooked.

"She is interested in you, Dan."

"Certainly she is. Isn't she interested in any man who won't fall and worship at her feet?"

Prescott ignored the bitterness. "I have never seen Betty as she has been since you came. She laughed and told me frankly you disapproved of her in every way. Yet behind the laughter I saw tears of hurt."

"You are imagining things!" Even as he denied the possibility, Daniel's heart took an uncontrolled leap. "I ask you again, can you imagine Miss Courtland working alongside me as any helpmate would have to do? Living in semipoverty? Bearing my children?" His laugh was harsh. "She could never do it."

"I think you underrate Betty. She has never had the chance to show what she could do under stress. She's been dandled and petted and just about ruined by permissive parents who never denied her anything she wanted."

"You are championing your fiancee as a fit companion for me?" The incredulity in Daniel's voice sent a wave of red to Prescott's hairline.

"You think I would go ahead and marry Betty, knowing her heart is not mine?" Prescott stared at this friend. "I have known all along she did not love me, although she is fond of me. It took seeing her look at you to expose the truth. I want no woman who cannot look at me in that same way."

Wordlessly Daniel held out his hand to be seized in a mighty grip and said, "I will go away. I know that I will find peace in doing my heavenly Father's will. She is young. It is a passing fancy, even if it should be as you say, which I doubt. I think she is merely intrigued because I don't bow down to her wishes." He ignored the protest in his friend's face. "She will see you as the man you are." For a moment his face twisted in agony. "Prescott, most men would hate me. It takes great love for a friend to accept what you have just done."

"Why should I hate you? If it hadn't been you, perhaps it would have been another man — after we were married." The somberness of Prescott's voice cut into Daniel like knife blades.

"I would stake my life that once she marries she will be true."

"If she marries the right man." Prescott's quiet statement sounded in Daniel's ears like a death knell. "It will never be me." Before Daniel could reply Prescott deliberately changed the subject. "The opening at the church has not yet been filled. It isn't too late for you to change your mind and accept it. Why don't you think about it some more?"

"God has called me to Pioneer."

"Perhaps. Yet how do you know He isn't calling you here to Grand Rapids first? You believe this God of yours directs those who trust Him. How do you know your coming here at this particular time isn't for a reason? How do you know Betty isn't meant to be your companion? With her finances and your ability to preach, you could build this church to gigantic proportions. Perhaps God knows that. Perhaps this whole thing has been planned."

Daniel's shoulders slumped. "I have thought of it — often — especially since I met Betty." He sounded tired. "Prescott, I want you to know that I have fought against this strange attraction, this spell she seems to have woven about me. You know the only times we've been together have been when you were unavailable. Each time the unsuitableness of anything ever coming about between us has been thrust home to me sharply, even if it hadn't been for you! She is absolutely heathen. She believes in nothing except her own pleasure. Can you imagine her ever becoming a 'Mrs. Minister' as my own mother was?"

"I still believe you are seeing only the surface. Underneath all the society whims and fashions, Elizabeth has depths that are as yet unexplored." Prescott stood abruptly. "Will you consider what I have said?"

"How can I help it?" The cry burst from Daniel's lips without warning. "It would be better for me to go away tonight and leave this temptation. Surely that is what it is, the last great temptation before I enter the work I have been called to do."

"Perhaps not. Perhaps it is something far different." Prescott halted in the doorway, his face lined and suddenly old. "I am breaking the engagement with Elizabeth tonight. You must decide what you want to do, what you must do. But it will not change my decision." Suddenly he looked young again, younger than Daniel had seen him since college days. "I have already arranged to finish my studies and become the lawyer I have wanted to be since I was small."

"Thank God for that!" Again the two men

gripped hands. "But what about your mother?"

A gleam came into Prescott's eyes. "I believe that when she knows Elizabeth and I are not getting married and coming to live here, she will find she isn't so ill as she thinks.

"By the way, Dan, whether you decide to take the Grand Rapids church or not, they would like you to preach before you have to leave. I told them I was sure you could fill the pulpit this coming Sunday."

"I don't know whether to bless you as a friend or tell you to get thee behind me, Satan," Daniel warned. "You seem quite able to arrange my life." He joined Prescott in the hall. "I hope when you think this over you won't regret it. How will Miss Courtland take it when you tell her?"

"You needn't worry. She'll think it was her idea." A curious look crept into his face. "Actually it is. I'll give her an opening by telling her I'd like to postpone the wedding since I want to get into law."

"You think she'll accept that?"

Prescott turned sober. "She will have to." Steel infused his voice. "Now that I've made my decision, I wonder that I didn't do it long ago. Funny thing, somehow I feel freer than I have in a long time." He flexed his arms in a sweeping motion. "I can hardly wait to get into a different atmosphere, one where I can work. Even Elizabeth and the prospect of travel with her couldn't quite drown the dreams I had to bury because of Mother." He was halfway up the stairs before he turned back, lit by a kindly sunbeam from the skylight above. "As for hating you —" He lifted his hands helplessly. "No regrets, Dan." He disappeared from sight, leaving Daniel standing at the foot of the stairs wishing desperately he could cry.

Slowly Daniel made his way into the garden, swallowing the lump that persisted at the gallantry of Prescott Wetherell, a prince among men. But it did not solve his own problem. It only compounded it. If Prescott had been angry, it would have been easier. He could have packed and gone, leaving part of his heart and many regrets. But not now. He had to face what might lie ahead.

Can Prescott be right? After all my plans, being so sure God wants me in Pioneer, can God be using Elizabeth Courtland as an influence to keep me in Grand Rapids? In spite of himself his whole body thrilled with remembrance of her beauty. *What if she can be led to the Lord? What a wife she would make!* A tide of red swept into his face. *What right have I to consider such a woman? Betty would never be the choice God has for me. She couldn't be. She is shallow, selfish, spoiled. Yet haven't other shallow, selfish, spoiled people turned over their lives to the Lord and gone on to become noted servants?*

"Nonsense!" He viciously thrust his toe against a rock, sending it flying, relieving some of his frustration. "She couldn't be part of God's plan in my life!" Yet the words of his friend had sunk deep.

Just ahead lay a green bower, private, encased by hanging vines and weeping trees. He had spent time there when he first came to the Wetherells. Now he automatically parted the curtaining branches and stepped inside. There was a carpet of green, bordered with flowers, a small bench. Unerringly he headed for it, dropped to his knees, and buried his head in his hands. His Gethsemane had come.

"Oh, Lord, this girl is everything against You. Why did I have to meet her? Why did I ever come here — to disturb Prescott's life?" The low cry seemed to stay on the ground. "Are You there? Is it possible Prescott could be right? Are You telling me to change direction, to accept this church at least for a time?"

Hours later Daniel Spencer rose from his

knees. He had received no change of orders from his Commanding Officer. He would preach as Prescott had arranged, then leave for Pioneer immediately. Betty Courtland would remain. She was not for him. Yet deep inside his soul was the cry, *Help her, God, to find Christ — and happiness — even though it can never be with me.*

"Mr. Prescott's downstairs." This time Abbie's face was lit with smiles. "Says he won't keep you long but needs to see you."

"How tiresome!" Betty stuck her foot into her slipper and pushed back her hair. "It's almost dinner time. Why should he come now?"

"It wasn't my place to ask," Abbie said primly. "But he's waitin' for you in the little sittin' room."

"Oh, Abbie, why didn't you show him into the library?"

The maid's face set in stubborn lines. "He asked to go into the sittin' room. Said when you came down he didn't want to be disturbed."

Was it fear that shot through Betty? It must be very important for him to come at that hour. How could he get away from his mother? Her lip curled, her confidence returning. Probably some trivial matter about the wedding. She tightened her fingers into fists. Very well. It was the perfect opportunity. She would tell him she no longer wished to be engaged.

She did not get the chance.

"Sit down please, Elizabeth." Betty looked at him in surprise. Seldom did he take such a solemn tone when addressing her. The usual good-natured Prescott seemed eclipsed by a stranger. Whatever had happened? Was Daniel — her heart lodged in her throat.

"Nothing has happened to — anyone?"

"Yes, Elizabeth. Something important has happened."

Betty narrowed her eyes as he continued.

"I have decided after all to pursue the career in law I have wanted for so long. I realize that will upset your plans, especially about the wedding. If you choose to break the engagement, I will understand."

It was the last thing she expected. She could only stare. She could hear the clock ticking away seconds in their noisy rhythm before she could get her voice. He was offering her the chance she had wanted. Incredible! "Th— there's another girl?"

Strange how his amused laugh reminded her of Daniel Spencer. "Hardly. I will be busy with law. It will take some time to get established the way I choose to do. I don't intend to rely on my family name and reputation. I intend to do it on my own."

Something more like respect than she had ever had for him flooded Betty's mind. "I think you should, Prescott." She dropped her lashes. "I also think you're right about breaking our engagement. After all, you'll be busy, and I'm not the type to sit at home without escorts while you're playing lawyer —" She swept a look upward that had always brought fire to his eyes. Not this time.

"Don't play games, Elizabeth."

The command in his voice, as unexpected as a bite from a pet dog, startled her. "Games? I?"

"Yes, you." He was smiling much as her father would smile. In the few minutes since she had entered the little room Prescott seemed to have added inches to his stature, years to his age. For one moment she felt he had grown beyond her and almost frantically clutched at the familiar. "But Prescott, you just said —"

"I said don't play games. You aren't in love with me. You never have been. It's all been arranged, convenient."

Betty's mouth flew open. "Why, Prescott dear, how can you even think such a thing? I've always been fond of you." Her protests died. "Or is it that you don't love me?"

To her amazement Prescott did not answer immediately. Instead he stared at her as if seeing her for the first time. Again she was uncomfortably aware of the similarity between him and Daniel. The thought flared her into action. "Is it because of Daniel Spencer? That's it, isn't it? He has turned you against me." Two tears of fury sparkled on her lashes.

Prescott threw back his head and laughed. It shocked Betty more than anything else could have done. Prescott was laughing at her! She rose defiantly, haughtily. "I believe I do not care to speak with you any more, Mr. Wetherell."

Prescott caught her hand, forcing her back into her chair. The laughter still tugged at his lips. "Elizabeth, I wouldn't have believed it. Yes, Dan Spencer has had something to do with this. In fact, he has had everything to do with it. You're in love with him."

Changing from rosy red to snowy white, Betty's face was a study in emotion. "How dare you say such a thing!"

"Because it is true." The finality in Prescott's voice silenced Betty. "Can you look me in the eye and swear you are not in love with him?"

She turned her head away indignantly. "Why should I? How could anyone care for a country lout like him? Are you insane?"

"No, Betty. Just glad I know the truth." He paused. "You asked if I still love you. I am not sure. I have cared a long time, always knowing deep inside it was not returned. Now — I just don't know." He rose to tower over her, a stranger from the Prescott she had played with since childhood. "I believe you could find a great deal of happiness if you would change and be the woman Daniel Spencer needs."

Betty desperately grasped for the reins of control. "Why should I change? I could never fit in his world even if I did care, and why you should think I do is a mystery to me!"

"He would never fit into your world. You would have to go to him."

Betty escaped from her chair, feeling as if she had to get out of the room before she went into hysterics. "Of all the improbable situations! My fiance of a few weeks comes to tell me he wants me to break our engagement — and follows it up by recommending I change my whole life in order to qualify as a fit bride for his best friend! Prescott, have you been reading too much fiction?"

Prescott gathered up his hat and coat

from a nearby rack. "I will expect to see a formal withdrawal of our engagement in tomorrow's papers. Good night, Elizabeth." He stopped just inside the door. "If ever you need help of any kind, come to me. I'll be there." The door opened and closed. He was gone.

"Prescott!" Betty threw wide the door and hurried after him. "Did you — does Daniel know — is he — ?"

"He knows I came here tonight and why. Good night."

Betty pressed cold hands against her flushed face. Could the scene she had played in the little sitting room be real? It was real. Prescott stood watching her, waiting for her to speak. As in a trance Betty saw herself strip off the ring with the heavy stone and lay it in his hand. "You might as well take this."

"Thank you, Elizabeth." This time she did not run after him. Instead she stood slowly watching a part of her childhood walk away, head up, chin high. The fingers of her right hand involuntarily felt for her third finger, left hand. How bare it seemed — but how light. Suddenly she was glad. It was over — the sham engagement she had hated. She was free.

No, she was not free.

Prescott's words haunted her. "You're in love with him."

He had not said Daniel cared for her. Hot and cold by turns, Betty forced a smile and entered the dining room. It would be time for dinner soon. She must prepare herself to tell her parents the engagement was broken. Yet why did it not seem a staggering task? All she could think of was Daniel Spencer. In love with him? Absurd. Was it possible the trap that she had laid had sprung, catching herself instead of her prey?

She pushed back all thoughts of Daniel when her parents entered. Once they were served and the maid gone, she tossed out her news. "I broke my engagement to Prescott tonight." Her voice started out small but gained assurance. "He is going into law, and I don't intend to sit around and wait until he gets around for a wedding."

The effect was shattering. Her father's wine glass came down with a little crash. Her mother's lips compressed in a thin line. "And just what do you intend to do?"

Betty looked up, surprised, "Just as I've always done. Have a good time." Catching the flabbergasted look on her mother's face, she added airily, "There are more fish in the sea and better than have ever been caught. I won't have any trouble replacing Prescott."

"You had better watch your step, miss." Betty was alarmed at the purple color tinging her father's face. "I'm getting tired of your flirting and carrying on. Pretty soon no decent man will have anything to do with you!"

"Then I'll find someone who will." Stubbornness matched stubbornness in father and daughter as they glared at each other.

"Hush. Here comes Sally with dessert," Mrs. Courtland warned. A strained silence fell until the maid left the room.

"I won't have it, I tell you!" Mr. Courtland thundered. "I thought you were finally going to settle down and do what any self-respecting young woman would do — marry and have children. There will be no more of this dilly-dallying, Elizabeth. You will marry Prescott Wetherell as planned and on the day planned, or I'll know the reason why. I won't have you single any longer, driving men to distraction. When you were younger it was amusing. Now it isn't. You will marry Prescott!"

Betty sprang to her feet, knocking over her water goblet. "And I say I shan't! You may be my father, but you can't marry me off the way you'd sell a prize horse. I am a person. I have rights."

"Rights? You have nothing except what I

give you!" Mr. Courtland's rage increased. "Do you have some other good-for-nothing on the string?"

Death itself could not have kept the rich blood from coursing into Betty's face. Her father saw it and jumped to conclusions. "Who is it? Who is he, the dishonorable man who would make love to you even while you are engaged to another man?"

"He has never made love to me. He despises me!"

Her father did not even hear. He brought down his fist to the heavy table with such force the silver jumped. "I demand to know his name, the man you fancy, or you will be locked in your room until you regain your senses!"

"I refuse to be treated as a child!" Betty stormed. "I told you there is no one who has tried to come between Prescott and me. Can't you understand? Prescott himself sees we could never be happy." It was her trump card. If it did not work, nothing would. She had seen her father in spells of rage before but never directed at her. She clutched the table edge with fingers white at the knuckles. "Will you listen? *Prescott asked me to break the engagement!*"

If her father had been enraged before, now his fury knew no bounds. His roar could have been heard throughout the Courtland mansion. "Then if that is true, and I will make it my business to find out, it must be because he knows you are unworthy to be called a Wetherell." He shoved back his chair with an oath, overturning it in his haste to get out of the room.

"Go to your room and stay there. I mean to have a talk with Prescott, and when I come back —" he shook his fist at her "— God help you if you have done anything that will reflect on the name of Courtland!"

White-faced, degraded by his accusations, Betty could not defend herself. Her own father, charging her with sins she could only guess at! She turned, walked up the stairs, entered her room, and locked the door. Let him rage and question. Her heart was as dead as if it had been pierced by a bullet. How could he believe some terrible thing of her? Sobs rose, shaking her entire body, but not one tear came. Her grief was too deep for tears.

What would Prescott say? Fear greater than shame flooded her body. What if some chance word caused her father to believe that Daniel Spencer — she could not finish the thought. Her father would never accept the innocence of their friendship, not now. He would seek Daniel out and either horsewhip or kill him. If there were a God, how could He permit such a horrible thing to happen? In her confusion Betty vaguely sensed it might not be God's fault, but her own. There was no time to think of it now.

She snatched up her bell, ringing it furiously, and admitted Abbie into her room moments later. "Get out my driving things and have the small carriage brought around." She forstalled Abbie's protest. "*Don't argue.* It's a matter of life and death!" Her fumbling fingers were already busy with fastenings.

For once Abbie did as she was told. The look in her mistress's face had been awful. But she was adamant when Betty was ready. "I am going with you." Nothing could change her — neither threats nor pleading. "Come on, Miss Betty. If it's life or death you can't stand there arguin' with me."

The next instant they were racing down the servants' stairs, out into the night. Without waiting for Sam's assistance, Betty climbed into the carriage and snatched the reins, giving Beauty an unaccustomed touch. Beauty snorted and leaped ahead, taking the corner at incredible speed. Abbie held on and braced herself, wisely asking no questions.

A tiny voice resounded in Betty's brain.

What if you are too late? What if he is dead? It will be your fault. Deep inside a cry too faint to reach her lips formed, winging its way to the pitiless stars above. *Please, if You're there, don't let me be too late.*

5

Betty reined Beauty sharply to the right and groaned. "Oh, no. Father's already there." Her stricken face stood out sharply in the gloaming. "Abbie, I'll hop out. You drive Beauty around where she can't be seen when my father comes out." Leaving no time for protest, she slowed Beauty, threw the reins at Abbie, and disappeared around the side of the Wetherell mansion.

She could not go in the front door. In all likelihood, the men would be in the library. If only she could have reached there first. Her mind raced faster than her feet as she crept close to the library window. She had to get inside, just in case anything were to happen. Wait! Prescott had showed her a tiny alcove off the library, barely room for one person to study. It was hidden from view by heavy curtains and had a door to the main hall. On feather feet she slipped further around the house to a side door where she could sidle through. Luck was with her. Moments later she had entered the alcove and hidden behind the curtains, holding both hands over her mouth to still the heavy breathing. From her vantage point she could see Prescott and Daniel slumped in chairs before the fire. Her father was nowhere in sight. Dare she call out and warn them?

She hesitated, and in that split second lost her opportunity.

"Mr. Courtland, Mr. Prescott." The wide library door swung open. The impassive butler ushered in her father and went out, closing the door behind him.

"Why, Mr. Courtland!" Surprise was evident in Prescott's face. "My father is not at home this evening."

"I came to see you." Courtland wagged his head toward Daniel. "Who's he?"

"Didn't you meet my friend Daniel Spencer the other night? Sorry. Daniel will be filling the pulpit this Sunday."

Eyes like steel drills bored into the young minister. Behind her sheltering curtain Betty rejoiced to see that Daniel did not flinch. "So *you're* the fellow who's turning down our offer to build some ramshackle church in the far West."

"That's me." Daniel's smile was disarming.

"Humph!" Courtland turned back to Prescott. "I'd like to speak to you, alone." His voice was ominous, and Betty shuddered.

"Certainly." Prescott raised his eyebrows and motioned to Daniel. "You can go out through the alcove if you like."

Betty froze to the spot as footsteps, quick and light on the heavy carpet, neared her hiding place. A strong hand swept back the curtains. Her eyes pleaded with the man who stood there looking down at her, terror evident in her clasped hands. Hesitating only a moment, Daniel stepped into the alcove and drew the curtains behind him. He could not step forward. Betty was in the way. Neither could he stay in his ridiculous position, half in, half out of the alcove. He motioned toward the exit door, and Betty shook her head violently. She could see the contempt in his face for one more "Madcap Betty" trick. Hot color filled her face, but she grasped his arm, pulling him to the bench beside her.

Daniel's lips opened to speak. She put her hand over his mouth and shook her head again. She could feel his heart beating as she crouched beside him on the tiny bench, gently pulling her heavy skirts back, thankful they were not rustling.

"My daughter tells me you are not getting married." Her father's accusation stilled the two eavesdroppers.

"That is correct." Betty shifted and

moved the curtains an inch so she could see into the library. The same strong hand that had opened the curtains gripped her shoulders hard, pulling her back from sight. Her father was facing the alcove. He evidently had not seen the movement. "May I inquire as to the reasons? Elizabeth has said that you asked that she break the engagement. That tells me that you have found out something to her discredit. If it is so," he pounded his heavy cane against the floor, "if it is true, I will cut her off without a cent!"

In that moment Prescott Wetherell was magnificent. Rising to his feet he glared icily into the eyes of Mr. Courtland. "How dare you doubt your daughter's honor?" Contempt shone in every pore of his skin. "Elizabeth Courtland may be high-spirited and full of mischief and fun, but she is the soul of honor! She would rather die than demean herself in any way!"

The granite face did not change. "Then why have you asked her to release you from your betrothal plans?"

"Because neither Elizabeth nor I would ever be happy together. I am going on to become a lawyer. I have always known that she loved me as a brother, not as a husband."

"Rubbish! It is not for women to say whom they shall love. Love comes to them after marriage, at least to nice women!"

The fire died from Prescott's face and he dropped heavily into a chair. "I regret to say I disagree entirely. Elizabeth and I have drifted with the tide of yours and Mrs. Courtland's and my parents' plans. Now we must choose our own lives."

"My daughter will do as I say! And I say she must have some other reason, or she wouldn't have agreed to break the engagement. I demand the name of the man!"

Betty turned pale as death, and the arm cradling her tightened, sending a surge through her like nothing she had ever known. Prescott's infrequent kisses had been almost brotherly and had meant nothing. Now the touch of this man threatened to undo every shred of pride she knew. It was all she could do from flinging her arms around him, begging him to hold her so forever.

Prescott's voice roused her from the daze she was in. "Do you dare to insult your own daughter?" His indignation knew no bounds. Tall, strong, he snatched Courtland by the lapels of his coat. "I will not allow you to stand in my home and speak such vile things of Elizabeth! You should be thanking God she is pure and clean instead of what you are thinking! Then you should go home and get down on your knees to her and apologize."

"Apologize? I? I never apologize. It's a sign of weakness." Courtland's face was purple again, veins standing out. He jerked free and stepped back. "I'll have the name of the man, and when I get it, I'll kill him like I would a snake that threatened my home!"

Prescott's face was nearly as dark as Courtland's. "What if Betty were guilty of unspeakable things? Whose fault would it be? What have you ever given her except her own way? Have you taught her to believe in God and respect Him? Have you given her any reason not to do what she chooses? Have you commanded respect by your own life or demanded it because you are a Courtland?" The words hurled themselves like bricks, each striking harder at the hypocrite facing him.

"I suppose your parents have done better?"

"No!" Prescott, who never swore, uttered a rough oath. "But I am learning that life is more than prestige and money and what 'they' think. I pray to God that I will one day become the man I'd like to be."

"Like the preacher who was in here?" The sneer on Courtland's face darkened. "A white-livered coward who will spend his life preying on weak-minded women?"

Betty's gasp was lost in Prescott's reply. She had never seen him look so, face flaming with passion. "If I can ever become half the man Daniel Spencer is, I will be thankful."

"Bah! I will continue this no longer." Courtland whirled toward the door, then back as a new thought struck him. "Is this minister interested in my daughter?"

"If he were, it would be the greatest compliment any woman could be paid. But why should he be? Outside of a pleasing personality and a pretty face, what could Elizabeth offer a man like Daniel Spencer? He needs someone who can stand up to life, not a pampered doll like your daughter. She would have fit into my plans, but never his."

"That will be all, sir!" Courtland advanced, cane raised.

"Yes, it will be all." Prescott reached for a pull rope and waited for the butler. "Show Mr. Courtland out. It is quite past time for him to go."

Courtland muttered incoherently and stomped after the butler, but paused to say, "You will regret this little conversation for the rest of your life. I will see to that!"

A curious tranquillity filled Prescott's eyes, lifting the corners of his mouth in a half smile. "Such is the reward for believing in your daughter, sir — the thing you should have been doing. If I had agreed with you, would you have killed me for insulting her?" Only the closing of the door answered him, its slam muted by its well-oiled hinges.

"Quick, you must go!" Daniel was on his feet, pulling Betty up.

He was a fraction of a second too late.

"Dan? You there? I thought I heard movement —" The curtains were thrown back, revealing the shrinking Betty and white-faced Daniel Spencer huddled in the tiny space.

"Elizabeth!" Was it the realization that she had overheard the whole thing that sent the deathlike look over Prescott's face?

Elizabeth finally found her voice. "I came — he said terrible things to me at home — I was afraid —"

"There really was no way out without her father discovering her," Daniel added as he helped her into the library itself. "I regret to say that any other alternative was out of the question."

"You heard it all? His accusations?" Prescott's eyes were filled with shame for her father.

"For the second time. He hinted at things I don't even know about at the dinner table." She looked up at Prescott. "If I knew how to thank you, I would."

"Don't!" The fierceness of his exclamation cut her off. "To think that you had to listen to that! It is despicable."

"But why did you come here?" Daniel interjected.

"I had to. I didn't know what he might do, if he found out I — we — that you had been seeing me."

Color swept to Daniel's hairline. "He thought what he wanted to think without any cause whatsoever?"

"Yes." Betty's head drooped like a flower, too tired to look up. "If he had known that Prescott had sent you to take me places, I don't know what he would have done. So I came here."

"Family pride like that," Prescott said, his voice cold. "Inexcusable!"

Daniel looked deeply into his friend's eyes. "Did you mean what you said about wanting to find your place in life — with God?"

"I never meant anything more." Prescott's gaze was steady, unshakable, leaving Betty feeling as if a charmed circle had been drawn around the two men, shutting her out. It hurt unbearably.

"Daniel, take Elizabeth home. She can

slip in without her father knowing." Prescott was in command, but Betty shook her head. "Abbie's waiting outside." Before they could stop her she slipped back through the alcove, out the door, and back to where the carriage stood with a trembling Abbie holding the reins. A minute later the two men in the library heard Beauty's hoofbeats as she slowly turned toward home.

"Hard lesson for her." Daniel poked up the already blazing fire, his face in half-shadow.

"Maybe it was what she needed. She's been known for some of her madcap ways. It's time she learned that there is responsibility in life."

"To what *they* think?" Daniel's lip curled.

"No, to herself." Prescott dropped back in a chair. "Daniel, I believe that Betty is capable of being another Mrs. Minister if she had direction and guidance such as you could give her."

"Never! I don't even want to discuss it!"

But long after Prescott had said good night, his guest remained in the library, remembering his decision earlier in the garden. As he watched a final spurt of fire before it died into ashes, he recalled how his heart had lurched at the softness of Elizabeth Courtland in his arms.

"I don't feel like going to church this morning."

"You're going." Mrs. Courtland was grim. "That friend of Prescott's has been filling Prescott full of wild stories. Your father says we're going to find out what it is about him that has hypnotized a person like Prescott into becoming an absolute boor!"

Despite Betty's misery at the thought of facing that same minister, especially in a preaching capacity, her lips twitched. *So Father thinks Prescott a boor, simply because he defended me. Perhaps the day will not be so bad after all.*

First Church was in for a shock — a series of shocks. The first came when Daniel Spencer entered the pulpit wearing an ordinary business suit instead of a clerical collar. "The idea," Mrs. Courtland hissed in Betty's ear. "If he thinks he can come in and start wearing that kind of clothing he might as well get it out of his head. We want no minister who can't respect God enough to dress properly!"

"Sh!" Betty could feel disapproving glances. There was no use reminding her mother that Daniel Spencer had no intentions of being their minister, even though they did not attend frequently. She was glad she could see him without being seen. A large woman in front of her screened her, but Betty could lean slightly and see around.

"*All* have sinned and come short of the glory of God." His Scripture reading was electrifying. "*All* we like sheep have gone astray." Several of the members who were prone to doze through the service for the sake of putting in an appearance shook themselves and sat up straight. This young upstart dared come in *their* church and read Scripture in that manner, emphasizing *sin?* It took the well-prepared anthem by the highly trained choir to soothe ruffled feathers. Perhaps he just had that way of speaking. Betty was reveling in the indignation around her, paying little heed to what was being said. Daniel certainly was speaking to those hypocrites in the church. Not once did it occur that ALL meant her as well.

The anthem was over. Now Daniel Spencer would step forward, congratulate the singers, and read a discourse. Betty settled back along with the others only to be shocked into uprightness.

"I will not be using the sermon I prepared." Each word fell clear-cut, like a stone plopping into the pool of silence. "I find that there is a message the Lord wishes me to bring in place of the one I had written out."

Never in the history of First Church had such a thing happened. Flags of color flew in Betty's eyes as she met Prescott's amused glance. Purple lights highlighted the deep blue. What was Daniel Spencer up to?

Folding his hands before him on the pulpit he leaned forward, then laughed lightly and stepped from behind the massive piece of furniture. "This is a beautiful pulpit, but it puts me too far away from you. It sets me apart as someone special, on a little higher plane." He deliberately stepped down from the platform to the floor in front and smiled again. "That's better. You know, this is what the Lord wants — for all of us to be closer together — and to Him."

First the Lord had a message; now he presumed to say what the Lord wanted. The congregation was paralyzed. It had been a long time since a minister had dared tell them the Lord wanted anything more of them than to attend on Sunday and drop a sum into the offering box. Yet there was not one person who did not lean slightly forward to meet whatever new thing would come next.

"You have asked me to fill your pulpit. You have asked me to accept a call to be your pastor, shepherd of your flock." He looked around, straight into the eyes of the disapproving board members who felt it out of place for him to discuss such things in church.

"I appreciate your invitation. Yesterday I spent a long time in prayer. I asked God what I should do about taking this church." Somehow his eyes seemed to have discovered Betty and were speaking to her. "When I came to Grand Rapids I knew I would not take this church. Yet, certain things happened that made me wonder; perhaps God had a work here for me to do."

In the little pause Betty's heart beat rapidly. Was she part of the reason he reconsidered? Joy flooded through her, only to be drowned by his next statements.

"I asked God what to do." The ripple was barely discernible, yet he caught it. "I always ask God what to do, and I hope you do too. It pleases our Father to give us direction." Again his eyes sought out Betty's corner.

"I asked Him if I should give up the plans I had to build a church in a little town named Pioneer, in the far West. It had been pointed out that perhaps someone else could best serve there and leave me free to serve you."

Betty's blood raced.

"Yes, I asked God. He said no."

Dumbfounded, Betty made no pretense at hiding behind the large woman. Along with the rest of the congregation she gaped at the man in the plain business suit who dared turn down their honored call so casually.

Something in his dark eyes called to her as he said quietly, "It was not an easy decision. It took struggle. The place I will go is far different from here. It will be small. I will often be discouraged by lack of numbers." Again he took a step toward the congregation. "As I prayed, the garden where I knelt faded. In its place was a small building that had once been a store. I never saw the building. I only heard of it.

"Years before I was born, a young man starting out his ministry felt called to start preaching the gospel in a little village on the Great Plains. He had been assured there would be those who would listen. What he had not been told was of the man who ruled the little village. The leader employed most of the people there or purchased their produce or in some other way controlled their living. He hated ministers. So when he found the former owner of the empty building had rented it to the young minister for a week, he was furious. He demanded the owner cancel the agreement.

"The building owner would not do so. He didn't care what the man thought; he was leaving for another town. The leader took another way. He visited people, and spread the word. No one was to attend the church service. If they did, there would no longer be a market or a job.

"The people were appalled, but what could they do? They had no money to move on. So regretfully, families who had looked forward to the series of meetings stayed home. The building owner fell ill and was unable to attend.

"The young minister came in eagerly. He swept the building and built a fire. He even managed to find a few sprigs of green to decorate a bit. The stove smoked, and the fire went out; but he only laughed. It had taken the chill of non-use from the room, and the evening was pleasant. He opened every window wide, letting the good fresh air finish the task of ridding the room of its odors.

"When seven o'clock came he was surprised to find no one there. Had the notice been changed to seven-thirty? No, the notice on the door said seven. He waited. Five after, ten after, fifteen after. By seven-thirty, he realized the truth. No one was coming.

"Outside the window huddled the town leader, peering in, enjoying the young man's discomfiture. To his amazement the dejection suddenly turned to action. The minister found a hymn book among his possessions.

" 'Abide with me, fast falls the evening tide,' in a strong voice came rolling out the open windows, down the streets, into homes of poor people. Doors opened. People poured out. The order had been given for no one to attend church. Who could be singing like that?

" 'Touched,' the town leader pointed to his head and whispered as others crowded beneath the window just out of sight. But others came closer.

" 'What's he doin' now?' A glance inside confirmed the truth — the minister was offering an opening prayer.

" 'Lord, I thank You for this opportunity to meet with You. I pray that You will bless the reading and speaking of Your Word this night. Amen.'

"Another hymn, then the young minister picked up his Bible and read a Scripture. People peered in to make sure someone had not slipped inside. The room was empty except for the minister who had gone on and was preaching — *to an entirely empty room!*

" 'Who's he a-talkin' to?' someone wanted to know.

"The town leader could only shake his head, eyes popping. Not one of those men or women left his spot by the window. They were spellbound by the simple words about Jesus Christ that the minister spoke to an empty room.

"When he finished, the young minister sang another hymn, gave a closing prayer, and stepped from the pulpit and into the yard. He gave no sign his 'congregation' had all been in the yard.

" 'Service tomorrow night at seven,' he called cheerily. 'Good night.' Then he walked down to his boarding place."

The magnetic voice stopped. There was not a sound in the entire First Church.

Daniel Spencer again took up the story. "The next night the little building was packed. In the very front row was the man who had passed the word to stay away. When the service was over he was first to shake hands with the young minister.

" 'Tell me, why did you go ahead with your service last night when no one else was here?'

"The young minister gripped the man's hand and looked him straight in the eye. 'Sir, God was here. My appointment was with Him. If others did not choose to come, it did not release me from my appointment.' "

Again Daniel paused, his eyes sweeping the silent congregation. "Friends, that little building is gone now. In its place stands a church where over a hundred people worship every week. If it had not been for that young minister who kept his appointment with God, it would never have come to pass. Why should I care about a young minister who preached to an empty room long ago in a dusty town? Let me tell you why."

Betty drew in a shaken breath, gaze fixed on his face. It was illuminated, reminding her of the face of an angel in a treasured childhood picture she once owned.

"The man who ran the town, the man who tried to run the preacher out of town, and the man who was first to recognize truth when he finally heard it through the lips of a young man called of God, was my own grandfather." His eyes seemed to bore into the hearts of his listeners, searching, probing to depths hidden from all save God. "If I can reach even one person the way my grandfather was reached, I will have fulfilled my calling — and it must be in Pioneer that it starts."

Betty collapsed against the back of the pew, drained. But Daniel Spencer was not through.

"I could stop now and let you all leave thinking this is my calling, without applying it to your own lives. I tell you this day, each one of you is being called of God to exemplify His qualities in whatever part of life you occupy." He relentlessly turned toward the board. "You, sirs, are required by God to find the minister for this great church that *He* would have you have." He turned back to the rest of the gawking congregation. "There is not one man, woman, or child within the sound of my voice who is not being called just the same way to be the best. Whether businessman, lawyer, doctor, wife, mother, or student, God has a call for you. Find it. When you do, you will be of all people most happy and blessed."

Slowly Daniel Spencer walked to his place. The last song was sung. The benediction was given. The congregation spilled out on the sidewalk, some laughing self-consciously, denying by their mirth the validity of what was said.

"Theatrical claptrap!" Betty's father muttered.

"Too bad. He has such nice eyes. But that cheap emotional story about his grandfather —" Mrs. Courtland's eyebrows lifted, completing her opinion.

Betty stood in a sea of comment, most of it adverse. They were coming out of the spell cast by what had happened inside, ready to complacently go on living the way they always had. Was she?

"What do you think of him now?" Prescott managed to whisper before meeting Courtland's frown and melting into the crowd.

His words fell on empty air.

Hands over her traitorous heart, torn apart with feelings new and untried, Betty had fled.

6

"You aren't going without telling Elizabeth good-bye!"

Daniel Spencer's lips involuntarily twisted with pain, and he looked away from Prescott. "I have to." Moodily he stared through the window at the heavy curtain of rain. "In spite of everything within me crying out that it is wrong, I have learned to care a great deal for her. Seeing her again would solve nothing." He impatiently stepped to his trunk and tightened a fastening. "You can tell her I said good-bye."

"I'm not sure if you are taking the coward's way out or doing the honorable thing!" Prescott admitted. "Since you feel nothing could come of it, perhaps you're right, but I don't know what Elizabeth is going to do when she hears you've gone."

"She'll find someone else. She always has, hasn't she?"

"Until now. This time I'm not sure she will."

"Better to wound her vanity than have her build false ideas about being the wife of someone she could persuade to accept First

Church and fit right into society." He laughed shortly. "Except I don't believe First Church is quite so eager to have me take the pastorate since I spoke there!" He turned moody again. "I really am not sure why I ever came to Grand Rapids — to break your engagement, upset the Court- lands, or turn the congregation upside down?"

"Don't forget, Dan, if you hadn't come I would still have been on the society tread- mill. Now I have hard work to look forward to — and getting to know your God better."

A rush of feeling swept away Daniel's dark reflection as he clasped Prescott's hand. "That's true. It's worth everything to hear you say that." He cleared his throat of the husky note. "I know you don't want me to refer to it, but I have to, this once. I don't know when I'll be back, if ever. Prescott, you are the finest friend I have ever known, and the most understanding."

"Don't make me out a saint. I'll admit when I first saw how Betty watched you I felt some pangs. Yet as I honestly searched myself and her, I knew it wasn't you who had come between us. It was Betty — and me." That time he was the one to laugh, slapping Daniel on the shoulder. "Come on, or you'll miss your train. I wish you would, you know!"

Long after the train left the station, speeding west into a new and strange land that would swallow his friend, Prescott Wetherell stood on the platform watching. The next thing was to tell Elizabeth Daniel had gone. It was not going to be easy. He could not go to the Courtland home with things the way they were. He would have to send a note.

It was the hardest note he ever had to write. Short. He made no effort to soften the fact that Daniel had left without trying to see her.

Dear Elizabeth,
    Daniel Spencer left this afternoon for his assignment in Pioneer. He asked me to tell you good-bye for him.

                        Faithfully,
                        Prescott

Calling a servant, he ordered, "Deliver this to Miss Elizabeth Courtland and see that it goes directly to her, not into the hands of anyone else."

"Yes, sir." If there was curiosity behind the impassive face it was well hidden. Yet Prescott sighed when the man was gone. How would she take it?

He did not have to wait long to find out. Almost before his man could return, he heard flying hooves. Beauty! Through the library window he could see Elizabeth tumble from the carriage practically before it stopped, race up the path, and pound on the front door.

He was there to meet her. "Why, Elizabeth!"

She lifted her tearstained face to his. "Is he really gone? Without a word for me?"

It almost melted Prescott's reserve. "Come in, child." He led her to the library. "He said to be sure and tell you good-bye."

"Good-bye!" Betty choked over the word. "Was that all? Didn't he leave any other message for me?"

"What message could he leave?"

Betty lifted her head proudly. "He could have said — he should have — I don't know, but Prescott, he's gone!" Never had he seen her so distraught. Her dark hair was disheveled, her eyes hurt. "I'll never see him again."

"No, you probably won't." Prescott stepped closer, lifted her chin, forced her to look into his eyes. "Elizabeth, do you care that much?"

For the space of a heartbeat Betty thought of denying. What good would it do to tell

103

Prescott of the feelings that filled her? She could not lie. "I care."

His grip tightened, almost to the point of cruelty. "Why? Because he's the only man who never fell at your feet at first glance? Because he was a challenge?"

"No!" She wrenched free, eyes nearly black with emotion. "Don't ask me why I care! He's nothing — rude, boorish, a hick preacher with not enough sense to snatch First Church when it was offered to him on a silver platter! He thinks I'm a cheap flirt, without anything a man needs to have in a wife. But, oh, Prescott, why did he go without me?"

"You don't mean you would have gone with him! You, Elizabeth Courtland? I can't quite see you milking cows and keeping house and cooking for him." His sarcasm increased. "What could you offer such a man as Daniel Spencer?"

"My love."

It stopped him short. "You can't really mean you love him. You've only known him a few weeks. You're entirely unsuited to each other. Why, even Dan said he would never tell you how he felt because you could never be happy —"

"He said *that?*" Glory trailed in Betty's face like streams of water seeking the ocean.

"Forget it!" His command was sharp. "I never meant to let you know."

"Know what, Prescott?" Color stained her white face. "That — that he cares?"

"It doesn't mean a thing that he cares or that he was attracted to you. He'll go into Pioneer and someday laugh at the idea of ever having given you a thought. He'll find someone who will stand beside him in that wild land and be the helpmate he needs."

"No!" She flinched as if he had struck her.

Again he held her arms, pinioning her so she had to look at him. "Even if you could learn how to be a wife, the kind he needs, could you ever learn to know the God he serves?"

Betty stared into the demanding face, a Prescott different from the gay companion she had always known. At last her answer came. "No, Prescott, I could not." Seeing the disappointment that came into his face she cried, "How could I? I don't even know if there is a God!"

"You really think you could fill Daniel's life as he deserves?" He dropped her arms, eyes chilled.

"What difference does it make about his God? If he wants to believe it, so what? It doesn't change how he feels about me." She warmed to her subject. "If two people care about each other, none of what they believe needs to matter. I've money, plenty of it. My grandfather left it in trust for me. You think Daniel Spencer would stay in Pioneer if he knew he could have me by going elsewhere?"

"Didn't he know that before he left?"

"How could he?" Her angry flush should have warned him of the tantrum to follow. "I certainly did not tell him, and I hope you didn't!" Her scornful accusations were in sharp contrast to her earlier woebegone state.

"You honestly think you could ever win him away from what he thinks God wants of him?"

Betty's eyes blazed with anger. "God! I will fight God with everything in me for Daniel Spencer! He's the only man I ever wanted, and I intend to have him, regardless of the cost!"

"Elizabeth!"

She was adamant. "I mean what I say. If I had known sooner he was attracted to me, instead of disapproving the way he acted all the time, do you think he would ever have left without asking — no, without begging me to go with him?"

"So you will fight God for Daniel Spencer and turn him into a tame cat, the way you have done with men all your life." Arms folded, Prescott stated the case quietly.

"You needn't act like judge and jury. If there really is a God, He wants Daniel to be happy."

"I can't believe you think you could ever make him happy!"

Betty drew on her gloves as she stepped toward the door. "I cannot imagine not being able to make any man happy, if I choose. Even you, Prescott."

She was unprepared for his stern reply. "I wonder."

"I really must go. Abbie will be wondering where I wandered off to. Thank you for the information. I will use it — to the best of my ability."

"You should be turned over my knee and spanked. You are nothing but a spoiled, greedy child, snatching what you are told you can't have!"

"And you, Prescott Wetherell, are insufferable!" Anger turned her eyes to purple. "If you think I'm so terrible, maybe you'd better be thankful to that God of Daniel Spencer's you escaped me!" She flounced out, but not before hearing Prescott's quiet response.

"Perhaps I should."

Betty drove home slowly, heart pounding.

So Daniel cared! The instinct that had driven her, had taunted her to cling to him in the little study that day had been true. He cared! His lean, handsome face formed before her. His lips did not smile with mockery; they smiled with welcome. Closer, closer — "Beauty!" A near miss with a great branching tree when Beauty swung a corner too wide brought Betty back to reality. Somehow she managed to get home and to her room. It was no punishment being alone as her father had ordered. It was time to think and to plan.

He would write. When Daniel got to that forsaken place he would write, maybe even within a few days. Betty's heart leaped. What would it be like to get a love letter from Daniel telling her he had found out he could not live without her? All the censure he had given was forgotten in the knowledge he cared.

It was the beginning of a new era for Betty Courtland. Each day she eagerly awaited the mail, only to turn away heartsick. Invitations poured in by the score as well as notes, flowers, and candy from the string of admirers who had suddenly focused their attention on her. There were many showers, teas, and luncheons. But not one word from Daniel Spencer.

If only she had not quarreled with Prescott she could get news of Daniel from him. But she was too proud to do that, too proud to admit that she had not heard from the man who had gone away without a word.

One night she overheard her father and mother talking. At the top of the stairs she stood unseen but frozen to the spot when she heard her name.

"What's got into Elizabeth?"

"I'm sure I don't know!" Had her mother's voice always been so querulous? "I found her in the kitchen the other day actually watching the cook bake a cake! When I asked her what on earth she was doing, she just said, 'Maybe someday I'll have to bake a cake. I was just watching how it was done.'"

"Elizabeth bake a cake? What foolishness is she up to now? You don't suppose she's grieving over Prescott, do you?"

"Of course not! She never loved him. She's just moody."

"Maybe we should send her to my sister and brother-in-law in New York for the winter. I'm getting tired of her doldrums."

"I hardly think that is necessary, Mr. Courtland." Her mother's voice was icy. "I don't approve of letting a young girl travel alone, and I certainly can't be spared from my committee work to take her."

Courtland sighed. "She'll be twenty-one in a few months. I never thought my daughter would be an old maid!"

"Well!" Even without seeing her, Betty could imagine her mother bridling. "If she is, it is from her own choice. But I admit, something's going to have to be done about her. She's even been driving out to see Emma practically every week! It's one thing to give to charity, but to deliberately seek out the company of one's former cook —"

Betty missed the rest. Biting her lip in vexation she slipped back into her room and deliberately banged the door coming out. The conversation below ceased as she ran down the stairs. Yet she did not miss the scrutiny of her father at dinner.

"Elizabeth." His colorless lips seemed ill at ease forming words of kindness. "Are you ill — or anything?"

For one ghastly moment she stared, then her face chilled. "No, I am not ill — or anything. I have not been ill — or anything. I will not be ill — or anything."

"Silence!" The head of the house thundered. "I won't have you answering me back!"

Betty sprang to her feet. "Then don't ask questions that are little more than veiled insults. Ever since I broke off with Prescott

110

you have acted as if I were some wanton creature. Either I am your daughter and trusted as such, or I will no longer remain in your house!"

"Elizabeth!" Mrs. Courtland threw up her hands in horror.

"You will do as I say!" His heavy fist balled, and he glared at her with eyes gone suddenly red. "That broken engagement has never been explained satisfactorily. Until it is, you are suspect. Prescott Wetherell would not have asked for release if you had not brought it on by some action of your own!"

"I meant what I said, Father." Very pale, very calm, Betty stood up and walked toward the staircase. "I will not listen to such talk."

"Come back here." He pounded the table for emphasis.

"I will *not* come back." Under her breath she added, "Ever." Running to her own room she locked the door, ignoring the pounding and the sound of her father's voice demanding an apology a few moments later.

With fumbling fingers she threw open her wardrobe door, heedlessly snatching a few garments. How long it was until another knock came at the door she never knew or cared.

111

"Please, miss, it's Abbie." The whisper came through the keyhole. "I've brought you some dinner. Let me in quick before I'm seen."

Betty unlocked the door and Abbie slipped inside, carrying a tray. Her face was splotchy. "If I'm caught, I'll lose my place."

Betty stared at her — the maid who had been with her so long. "Abbie, I have to get away. My father has accused me of unspeakable things. Will you help me?"

Abbie gasped. "How can I help?"

"Carry out this carpetbag with my things under some towels, as if you had washing. Then get Beauty hitched to the light carriage. Sam will do it if you tell him, and do it quickly!"

"How will you get out? Your parents are still in the dining room!"

"I'm going out the window." Betty had been making rapid plans while she worked. Now she slipped from her long skirts and dropped them out the window. Slim, clad only in slips and shirtwaist, she whirled toward Abbie. "I'll climb down the big tree. Now hurry!"

It was easier than she had thought. The branches grew close, and she stepped from one to another, down, down. Once she almost fell as a limb broke but clung to the tree trunk and felt for safer footing. When she reached the bottom she put her skirt back on and headed around the house to Beauty and the carriage.

"Where will you go, Miss Betty?"

"It's better that you don't know. All you know is that you saw me drive away with Beauty. I'll get in touch with you when I can."

"Will you be all right?" Betty could see tears running down Abbie's freckled face, her hands clasped earnestly.

"I'll be fine. Remember, all you know is that I drove away." She gathered the reins and lightly touched Beauty with them. "Good-bye, Abbie — for now." Quietly the faithful horse stepped forward. Betty did not look back. The mansion she had lived in was already part of her past. Where could she go at this hour of night? A vision of an open hearth and bubbling stew rose before her. Emma! The little cottage would give her shelter until she could plan ahead. Money was no problem. Betty's legacy from her grandfather had come to her when she was eighteen. There would be more when she was twenty-one. She could stay with Emma until then and — no, it would be the first place they would look for her once they discovered she was gone.

The miles paced off under Beauty's hooves as she planned. A daring idea formed, was rejected, and came again, more insistent than before. What if she were to board the train and go to Daniel Spencer? When he learned her own father continued to think ill of her he would have to marry her!

"I'll go to Pioneer. He will feel sorry for me, know I have compromised my good name by running away. Once we're married I'll show him what the difference between his precious Pioneer and having me can be." She was almost surprised when she reached the darkened house she sought. Wild plans filled her head.

"Emma?" She pounded on the door and was rewarded by a sleepy voice. "Emma, it's Elizabeth Courtland. May I come in?"

"Miss Betty!" The old woman's face was a mass of wrinkles in the hastily lit candle. "You here, this time of night?"

"My father has cast me out. May I stay here with you until I know what to do?"

"Of course, lassie. But what's the trouble at the big house?"

"Because Prescott and I decided to break our engagement Father thinks I have done something dishonorable." It was out in words, and Betty cringed at the shock in old

114

Emma's face. "I haven't, Emma, I haven't!" All the emotion she had held back during that awful scene rushed over her. "Is it my fault that I don't love Prescott?"

"Or that you do love the other young man, Mr. Spencer?"

Betty dropped to a worn chair, head in hands. "Yes, I love him."

A hand, work-hardened, stroked her hair. "Don't cry. Does he love you?"

"He loves me but thinks I couldn't be a good minister's wife."

"Aye, I can see how he would feel that way."

"I can, Emma, I know I can. I can learn to cook and sew and everything else I need to know, can't I?"

"If you want to badly enough." She straightened from her crooning position over the young woman she had cared for since she had been a child. "Now, off to bed with you. Things always look worse at night."

Betty knew she could not sleep a wink. She was shocked to open her eyes and find morning had arrived. There was a great sore place inside when she thought of her parents, yet as all her plans rushed over her, joy overrode the sadness. The heavy porridge with cream heartened her for what lay ahead. Somehow she must get word to Abbie to pack her trunk. But why not take Abbie with her? If ever she chose to return it would be so much more respectable if her maid had gone along.

Just as dusk fell Betty quietly pulled Beauty up a short distance from her former home. Now if only she could attract Abbie's or Sam's attention. They adored her and would not tell. Luck was with her. In a brief time her father and mother walked down the steps. She could hear the rustle of her mother's skirts and her complaining voice.

"Really! I don't see why you didn't force Betty to open her door. The idea of letting her sulk inside for an entire day isn't my idea of how to tame her. You should have made her answer when you called!"

Betty's heart leaped. They thought she had been in her room all day!

"Let her sulk. She'll come out when she gets hungry enough. Now let's go. The Fosters hate to be kept waiting!" Her father passed close enough for her to have reached from the shrubbery and touched him. A pang shot through Betty, not for the cold man he was, but for the kind of father he might have been. What if he had been like Daniel's father?

Her reverie was interrupted by the carriage leaving. Now was her chance. They would be gone for hours. The Fosters held late parties.

"Abbie, Sam!" She sped inside, closing the door behind her. "Help me." Staring into their stunned faces she stamped her foot. "I said, help me! Sam, get my big trunk. Abbie, pack your clothes."

"My clothes!" Every freckle stood out on Abbie's face.

"Yes. I'm going to Pioneer, and you're going with me!"

Abbie fell back from Betty's advance as if she were a spirit. "Pioneer? Out West?"

"Must I do everything myself? Do as I say! Get everything you own that can be packed easily. We have to be out of here before my parents come back."

"But — but —"

"Don't you want to come with me?" Betty paused in mid-flight up the stairs. "I need you, Abbie." Her face suddenly looked old. "Mother and Father have made it impossible for me to stay. I'm going to Daniel Spencer." Her voice trembled, and it was not all acting. "If only you go, I will at least have one friend."

Abbie responded to the forlornness of her voice rather than the orders. "Then if you need me, I'll come. Hurry, Miss Betty, or we won't be away before the master comes back."

Incredibly they finished what was needed long before the Courtlands were due home. Betty even took time to hastily scrawl a note.

Daniel Spencer cares for me and I for him. I am going to him. Abbie is with me, so all is respectable.

She hesitated. Could she honestly sign it "With love?" Her lips tightened. She would not be a hypocrite. Scribbling the word *Betty* at the bottom she placed it in Sam's hands and disappeared into the night.

7

When Daniel Spencer waved good-bye to his friend Prescott it was with little hope that he would ever see him again. Grand Rapids was rapidly disappearing in the lurch and sway of the train that carried Daniel away. Where was the excited flush he had anticipated, the knowledge of carrying the gospel to those who needed it so much? For one moment he almost hated Elizabeth Courtland for ruining the special moment he had waited for for so long. If only he had never met her.

Fixing his lips in a grim line Daniel turned his eyes to the passing countryside. Rolling hills, farms, trees such as the one that had sheltered him when he and Betty had their long talk the first time they had driven together.

"God, have I been untrue?" He did not realize he had spoken aloud until the curious look from a man across the aisle brought him back to the present. Daniel leaned back against his seat. Why must he be tormented? He had fought his fight, set his course. Must he be haunted by shadowy eyes that changed from deep blue to purple, hair so dusky as to be part of the wraiths around him? Yet what a follower Betty Courtland would make, if her loyalty could ever be fixed on God. He dwelled on that for only a moment, then firmly pushed it aside. She was foreign to his faith, his belief, his work. He would not allow himself to moon like a stupid schoolboy.

The decision carried him miles toward his destination. After changing trains in Chicago he closed his eyes, little caring for the tall buildings. They would be part of his past.

Somewhere in the Dakotas Daniel roused to a voice. The conductor was entering his car calling, "Is there a doctor here or a minister?"

"I'm a minister." He sprang to his feet.

"Come with me, please. There's a lady dying and calling for a minister."

Daniel followed the conductor down the narrow aisle, clutching chair backs when the train swayed around a corner. It was not far — just two cars ahead. In the first car the conductor had found a doctor, a man not much older than Daniel but with lines in his face showing that he had seen much of life that was not pleasant.

"There, sister, what seems to be the matter?" The doctor's cheery greeting brought faint color to the white face of the patient.

"My heart. My physician warned me not to take this trip, but I wanted to see my daughter out West." The little old lady clutched her chest as another spasm of pain shook her.

Instantly the doctor was on his knees beside her. "Well, let's just have a listen." His stethoscope was already in his hand when he reached her. "Hm."

"It isn't good, is it?"

"No. I'm afraid your physician was right." The doctor's words were gentle in spite of their frankness.

"A minister?" Her faded eyes searched the area.

"This man's a minister, ma'am." The conductor respectfully stepped back for Daniel to approach her.

"I want to talk with him — alone." Her breathing was labored. Daniel glanced at the doctor and caught his look. The next moment he and the conductor were gone.

"I'm not afraid to die," the little lady told Daniel. "I just thought it would be nice — if someone said a prayer. I know God. He and my husband are waiting for me."

Daniel felt his throat tighten in response. He put one of his big hands over her frail one. "I'm sure they are. Why, they're probably getting ready for you right now."

"Could you —" she was growing perceptibly weaker. "Would you —" Her fingers clasped Daniel's strong ones.

"Dear Lord, welcome this child to Thy care. Help her to go with joy to meet You. Bless us all, for Jesus' sake, Amen."

"I'm glad you were here." She opened her eyes and smiled. "Tell my daughter I'll be waiting —" Her grip loosened.

It was a long moment before Daniel could get up from his knees and step into the aisle where the conductor and doctor waited. "She's gone." The doctor disappeared inside and returned shortly, nodding.

"She left instructions," the conductor told them. "Before she called for you she told me what to do."

Strangely silent, Daniel turned back toward his own car to be halted by the hearty grip of the stranger doctor. "Brother, would you like to talk a bit?"

Daniel measured him with his eyes, taking in the carelessly worn suit, the steady face. "Of course."

"I'm Gordon Stewart." He held out a well cared-for hand.

"Daniel Spencer." They dropped into Gordon's seat and the empty one next to it.

"Glad you were aboard. When there's nothing left for me to do, you people come in handy."

In spite of the little smile Daniel could feel his hackles rise. "Not just when there's nothing you can do."

"Sorry if I trod on your toes." The doctor's face looked weary. "I guess I just never could understand why men became ministers."

"Perhaps for the same reason you became a doctor." Daniel still smarted under the other's casual comments. "Why did you, by the way?"

"It's what I always wanted — to help people."

"My very reason for becoming a minister." Somehow Daniel found himself telling the stranger who was rapidly becoming a friend all the things that led to his accepting the call to Pioneer. Only once did Gordon Stewart interrupt. "You say you're going to a little dump in the Northwest to build a church? Why didn't you stay and work in some city church?"

"Why didn't you stay in some city hospital?" Daniel shot back. "You just told me you broke free because of rules and regulations — because you couldn't be free to practice medicine as you saw fit. Why should I be any different?"

Gordon's hearty laugh restored peace. "I guess you shouldn't. Tell me about this town of Pioneer."

The churning wheels ate up miles while they talked. Far into the night, their low voices vibrating with dedication to their chosen fields, they shared. Two who had come together by chance — or was it?

"Do you believe things just happen, or are they planned?" Gordon demanded at one point. "For instance, were you on this particular train because it led where you wanted to go? If so, why not a train a day earlier or a day later? If you were on for a reason, was that reason to be with the woman when she died, to comfort her? I overheard her telling you she was glad you were there."

Daniel's mind was racing. Did he dare say what he felt? Breathing a quick prayer for just the right words he leaned forward, intent on the thoughts coming with lightning rapidity. "Gordon." They had long since dispensed with formality. "What if I told you I believe I am on this train not because of her, although I was able to minister, but because of you?"

"To convert me?" Disappointment shaded the question.

"Not at all." Daniel flashed a smile. "That might be a side effect, but that isn't what I meant."

Gordon's suspicious glance did nothing to help the conversation. "Just what do you have in mind?"

"Why don't you go to Pioneer with me? There's no doctor there, but plenty of work."

"Are you out of your head, man? Why would I go to a place like that?"

"To help people."

The challenge lay between them, given, not yet taken up.

"I can help people wherever I go."

"But will they need it as much as the people in Pioneer?" Again Daniel leaned forward, deadly serious. The more he thought of it the more right it seemed. If only such a man as Gordon Stewart could be convinced to practice in Pioneer.

"I have the chance for a job in Seattle."

"Will it really be any different from the one in Chicago?" Daniel ignored Gordon's black look. "There are many doctors in Seattle. There are none in Pioneer." A thought crossed his mind. "Of course, if you are in it for the money —"

"Money? Never! I am a doctor because I have to be one."

Daniel took heart. "Then why not be a doctor where you are needed desperately? There are loggers in Pioneer who are brought into town injured, needing medical help. The nearest doctor is thirty miles away over rough roads that are barely passable. The nearest hospital is another twenty miles past that, again on roads that can become little more than ruts in winter. Sometimes trees are down. Women in childbirth have had babies while waiting for someone to clear a tree from the road. Some have lost their babies, simply because there was no doctor. The man who encouraged me to go to Pioneer told me all that. He also said that in at least seventy-five percent of the deaths, if there had been a doctor, the patients would have survived."

"A layman's opinion."

"Yes. But a qualified layman. He served as doctor's helper during the Civil War. He's too old now to be of much help, but does what he can." Daniel could feel defeat creeping through him. Why had he thought he could interest this man in Pioneer?

"Why do people live in such an isolated spot?"

Was there more than curiosity in the question? Daniel countered with another. "Why do people live in any particular spot? Because it's all they know — or where they make a living — or where they are sent by a Higher Power than themselves."

"And you believe I am being *sent* to Pioneer, as well as yourself?"

Daniel stood and stretched. The cynical smile on his new friend's face did not escape him. "I believe no man on earth can decide that for another. Good night." He turned on his heel and made his way to his berth.

It was not their last conversation about Pioneer. In spite of his unwillingness to even consider practicing there Gordon had an insatiable interest in the little town. He pumped every detail Daniel knew from him.

"Maybe I'm presuming," Daniel told him. "Perhaps you have a wife or family who would hate it there."

"No wife or family. The girl I loved died a few years back. I couldn't help — a congenital heart defect." Daniel saw the lines deepen into furrows and understood the look in Gordon's face. "So many others who seemed to have less to live for, and yet Susan was taken. Why?"

"I won't even attempt to answer that question."

"Good. I've heard all the platitudes about there being a reason." Gordon stared out the window. "I wonder if Susan would want me to go to Pioneer?"

"We'd make a good team," Daniel contented himself with saying, not allowing his exultation to leap into his face and be seen. It was too tremulous, too cobwebby a beginning. "Besides, the little railroad that goes in and out of Pioneer daily runs both ways. If you looked it over and decided against it, you'd still have time to take the Seattle opening."

"Maybe I will."

From then on the conversation was not of the past but of the future. Somehow, once Gordon made his decision to look Pioneer over, there did not seem to be any doubt in Daniel's mind as to the outcome. How could anyone, especially a doctor, see the need in a place like Pioneer and turn his back on that need?

With a start Daniel realized he had not thought of Grand Rapids or Elizabeth Courtland as he had thought he would do. In the face of what lay ahead, they receded into a dreamlike trance. Was it another lifetime that he had held her for the one brief moment in the little study, feeling her softness almost to the point of yielding? Now it seemed long ago, something that had nothing to do with Pioneer and Gordon Stewart. The country had changed from plains to mountains to desert and back to mountains. When they reached the small village where they would board the train for the last of their journey, Daniel was too full for words. There was a wooden platform with trunks piled high, a black monster, breathing fire and belching smoke, a high, clear whistle calling them on, and blue skies like he never before had seen.

Yet with every inch of those last miles Daniel could feel his nerves tighten. He refrained from looking at Gordon, who had grown silent. What would they find? In spite of all the preconceived ideas, even the country they traveled through was unfamiliar. Great stretches of untouched timberland passed before them. The train slowed as a buck, his doe, and two spotted fawns crossed the shining tracks that cut through their territory. Daniel and Gordon caught glimpses of mighty rivers and glistening streams.

"I'll bet there are fish in those streams." Gordon suddenly grinned at Daniel. "Of course if what you say is true, a man won't have much time for fishing — at least not my kind of fishing. Now, you are a fisher of men, I've heard tell. Wonder who might catch the most?"

Pioneer dawned on them before they were

quite prepared. They rounded the last curve, the whistle triumphantly announced their arrival, and it lay before them — a huddle of crude houses in a raw land. Carved from the forests that towered to the edge of what they called a town, Pioneer could by no stretch of the imagination be called inviting. Dust lay thick in what must be Main Street. It clung to a series of buildings that were the seven saloons Dan had told Gordon made up most of the "business." A little apart stood a ramshackle building marked General Store. Long benches on the porch gave evidence of visitors, as did the worn boards of the flooring.

"Whew! Not the most elegant place in the world!"

Daniel had expected crudeness. Still his heart sank. For himself it did not matter. Seen through Gordon's eyes, it was pathetic — this hamlet in the wilderness that *dared* call itself a town.

"What's that?" Gordon lifted his head as they stepped down.

A passerby called back over his shoulder, "Speeder whistle! Someone's hurt and comin' out from the logging camp!"

Forgotten was the sparsity of Pioneer. Before the speeder with the injured man stopped Gordon was there, black bag in hand. "I'm a doctor. Let me in here!" Daniel saw the bloodstained bandage around the man's leg and the agony of his face even as one of the loggers on the speeder said, "Widowmaker got him."

"Widowmaker?"

The logger looked at him scornfully. "Dead snag."

"Is there a place he can be taken?" Gordon addressed the same logger. "I've got to get this leg sewn up right away, or he'll bleed to death!"

"Bring him to the hotel." The big logger was already elbowing his way through the anxious crowd that had gathered. "Easy, there, men." Daniel was amazed at the gentle way the patient's comrades lifted the hastily improvised stretcher.

"You'll have to help me," Gordon told Daniel. "Had any experience?"

"A little." Daniel was already stripping off his coat and rolling up his shirt sleeves.

"Good." They beat the patient to the hotel. "You have hot water?"

"Sure, Doc." Someone must have run ahead. The hotelkeeper was lifting steaming kettles from his huge wood stove.

"Good." Gordon motioned to Daniel. "Bring my instruments as soon as they've been sterilized." He was already on his way

131

to the little room where the logger was biting his lips until the blood came to keep from screaming.

Daniel would never forget their introduction to Pioneer — the tense faces of the loggers, the only partially relaxed logger. What pain killers Gordon had could not work rapidly enough to spare him all the agony of the cleansing of the deep wound, followed by countless stitches.

"There. As neat a piece of stitching as I've done in some time." Dr. Stewart washed his hands and rolled his shirt sleeves down. "I'll just keep an eye on him and in a few weeks he'll be good as new."

"Thanks, Doc." The head logger had stood by for orders during the entire operation. "And thanks —" he looked at Daniel inquiringly.

"Daniel Spencer. I'm your new minister."

Blankness greeted his statement. "A preacher?" It was followed by a loud "ha, ha." "Well, you're shore a good one. Never knew a preacher before who'd jump in and help like you did today. Andy'll be pretty glad." His statement gave Daniel a lot of insight into just what kind of preachers those loggers had evidently known.

"Are there rooms we can rent here?" he turned to the hotelkecper.

"Shore. Don't s'pose you'll be stayin' long. They usually don't." It was further enlightenment on the status of religion in Pioneer. Daniel's jaw was set.

"I'll be staying."

"So will I." Gordon looked directly into the crowd of men. "Why isn't there a better place for injuries than here?"

The head logger's face turned a dull red. "No need for one. Didn't have a doctor. Why have a horspital?"

"You have a doctor now." Grim, steady, Gordon gathered up his instruments.

"Then we'll have to see about gettin' a horspital."

Was the man joking? Daniel shot him a glance and found something in the rough man's face that reassured him. It was no joke. It was as simple as that. If a hospital was needed, it would be provided. The beginning of warmth for the loggers in front of him stared out through Daniel's dark eyes. "Dr. Stewart needs a place while the hospital is being built. Is anything available?"

The leader scratched his head. "Well, there's the Smith shack. They up and moved off — said they weren't comin' back. It ain't much, but it has three rooms."

"Fine." Gordon held out his hand to be crushed in the other's grip. "Will you show us where it is?" He turned back to Daniel. "You're going to live with me, aren't you?"

Daniel hesitated. With patients coming in all hours of day and night, could he accomplish what he had come to do? Yet the Master he followed had taken care of the sick and helpless even before showing concern about their souls. "I will if you want me."

"Better stay here a few nights," the hotelkeeper advised. "That Smith place needs a good cleanin'. We can get some of the women to help, if you like."

"That won't be necessary." Daniel caught a glance of approval from Gordon. "I'll clean it while Dr. Stewart gets a room set up for his work."

"You shore ain't like the other preachers," one of the loggers commented, moving toward the door. "Well, my woman'll be glad to help, anyway."

"Ours, too."

But the logger leader stopped just inside the door, heavy calk boots scratching the already scarred floor. "Better take the help, preacher. Pioneer takes care of its own — and it 'pears like you 'n' the Doc are goin' to be part of us."

"Well!" Gordon turned back to Daniel when the others had gone, eyes sparkling with higher interest than Daniel had seen before. "In the words of our new friend, it 'pears we're goin' to find plenty to do in Pioneer."

"It also appears we'd better take a look at that Smith cabin. Might as well see what needs doing."

"Yeah, but let's go ahead and keep our room here until it's cleaned. I don't hanker to move into a place that's been left for the birds and squirrels. Wonder why the Smiths 'up and moved off'? Seems like quite a place to me."

"Then you have no regrets?"

Gordon's fine eyes darkened. "After seeing the need here? Who's going to have time for regrets?" He stepped through the door in the direction of the cabin that had been pointed out. "I have a feeling we're going to be two busy people for the next few months."

"I hope so." Daniel did not see the quick glance Gordon gave him. For one second only, he thought of the contrast between Grand Rapids, First Church, Prescott, and Elizabeth, and all they stood for rose to protest against the appalling primitiveness of Pioneer. The next moment he was following Gordon down the overgrown trail toward the Smith shack where they would create a semblance of a home.

"All it needs is a good cleaning," Gordon exulted. "I can take the biggest room for my office and the alcove to sleep. You can have the middle size room. There's even an extra door. You won't have to be bothered when patients come." He looked like a boy on a camping trip. "There's a fireplace, but I reckon we'd better eat at the hotel. I'm not much of a cook. Are you?"

"Not me! I can if I have to, but I hate it. Besides, since we don't have to rent rooms, the money can pay for meals." Daniel was catching some of his comrade's enthusiasm. "We can —" he broke off. "What's that?" A buzz like a swarm of bees was followed by a knock on the door.

"Why, hello!" Daniel looked over the small army of women. How had word gotten around so fast? Each was armed with broom, cleaning cloth, and pail of hot water.

"Shoo! Out of here." The foremost woman waved her mop threateningly. "When we heard there was a doc and a preacher in town we just grabbed our stuff and came. You git out of here so we can clean!"

"It really isn't necessary, Mrs. —"

"Sloane. My husband's head logger. Now git out of here, will you? You'll have plenty to do once you move in." A murmur of assent went through the crowd. "Oh, there'll be a potluck after church on Sunday, so you'll want to plan for it."

"Potluck? Church Sunday?" Gordon sounded as confused as Daniel felt.

"Shore. We got a preacher and a new doc, and we can use the schoolhouse. I hear tell as how there's goin' to be a new church, but no sense waitin' 'til the Lord sees fit for it to git done. We'll have preachin' Sunday."

Gordon and Daniel fled from the swarm, laughing all the way up the trail. "Well, so there will be church Sunday! I've had my introduction to Pioneer." Gordon's eyes danced. "Now it's your turn!" He turned back toward the station for their baggage. "I have to admit — I'm curious to see just what you choose to talk about in your first sermon in Pioneer!"

Daniel grinned a bit sheepishly. "Oh? You're not half so curious about that subject as I am. I get the feeling it's going to be quite an affair."

8

Daniel Spencer straightened up and rubbed his back. No sign of an ache. The hard days of work had toughened him. It did not seem possible that so much had been achieved in the short weeks since he had come to Pioneer.

Before him lay a low building, raw logs shining in the sun. Tom Sloane had been as good as his word. Every spare moment the loggers had pitched into work on their "horspital." Crude, compared with hospitals he had seen, it boasted four separate rooms, one of which Gordon Stewart would occupy.

"It's not that I haven't enjoyed bunking with you," he told Daniel. "This way I can be closer to my patients. You can have a little more peace and quiet for your work too."

Daniel smiled. The bond of friendship that had grown between the two was like the one he had shared with Prescott Wetherell. For a moment a pang stirred him. Prescott! In the busy days, working long after dark by the light of kerosene lanterns, he had managed to hold back thoughts of Prescott —

and of Elizabeth. He smiled again, grimly this time. What would she think of Pioneer? His mouth twisted. The very rawness of the place answered his question. She would hate it.

"Sorry I haven't been more help building," Gordon regretted. "Seems like every sick person in Pioneer just waited until I came. I even pulled a tooth the other day. The littlest Sloane boy had a swollen jaw, and Mrs. Sloane said she 'reckoned I'd better git it out' since they couldn't go to a dentist — takes too long." He grimaced. "Can't say I enjoyed that. What we need in Pioneer is a dentist."

"And a laundry. And a bakery. And a —"

"Hold it!" Gordon threw back his head and laughed. "Our town will get them all in time."

"Our town?" Daniel's eyes were dancing. "I thought you were 'jest stoppin' over fer a spell.'" He dodged the sweet-smelling wood chip Gordon hurled at him.

"Say, aren't they a grand bunch of people? I wish some of the earthborn snobs in cities could see how happily these people live — for the most part." He frowned. "Saturday nights are something else. The drunken sprees some of these men go on give me a lot of heads to patch."

"Isn't it strange." Daniel dropped to a stump, clasping both hands around one knee. "They fight Saturday night, yet most of them have been coming to the Sunday preaching. The other day Andy sidled up to me and slipped me a bill. He said, 'It ain't much, but reckon it'll help.' I've never known a freer-handed, more open-hearted bunch of people."

"I know." Gordon shaded his eyes. "Tom Sloane told me that just because the boys let off steam didn't mean they didn't want better things for their 'womenfolk.' He thinks your coming is one of the best things that's happened to Pioneer."

"Not to say anything about your own part," Daniel jeered. "I suppose Pioneer doesn't think a thing of your being here!"

"Don't fool yourself." Gordon struck an exaggerated pose. "I've never been so praised and appreciated in all my days of doctoring. Catch me ever going somewhere else!"

"Put 'er there." Two hard hands met in perfect understanding. "I wouldn't trade all of Pioneers's inconveniences for New York City itself."

"Or for Grand Rapids?"

The pressure of Gordon's hand increased until a weaker man would have cried out with pain. Daniel had long since told Gordon of Elizabeth Courtland and his opportunity to stay in Grand Rapids at First Church. "Especially not for Grand Rapids."

The next day Elizabeth Courtland and Abbie Tucker arrived in Pioneer.

It had been a long trip. Once they were successfully away from Grand Rapids some of Betty's glee diminished, but none of her determination. "We'll just enjoy the trip, Abbie," she confided. "I've got plenty of money. In the spring I'll be twenty-one, and then we'll have more than we'll ever need. I'm going to show Daniel Spencer that he's a fool to stay in a dump like that Pioneer must be." She fell to brooding, leaving Abbie wide-eyed, staring out the dirty train window.

Madcap Betty's plans were interrupted in Chicago. She and Abbie changed trains successfully after getting instructions from the porter. But when they were seated Betty gasped, "Abbie! My bag — it's gone!"

"Miss Betty! How could it be?"

"I remembered when we started up the steps that someone jostled against me." She frantically looked on the floor beside her. "It must have been stolen!" She turned a despairing face toward the freckle-faced girl who had begun to be more friend than maid on their trip. "What shall we do?"

"I have our tickets," Abbie reminded. "You told me to carry them. I also have a few dollars you gave me."

A little color returned to Betty's pale face. "Thank heavens! At least we won't be put off the train."

"You could wire back for money, couldn't you?"

Betty shook her head violently. "No. I secured all the money I could before we left. There will be no more until I'm twenty-one, and we have all this winter to get through." Her frown lifted. "Oh, I'm being ridiculous! Daniel will marry me as soon as we get to Pioneer. I won't have to worry about money at all." She went on, planning happily. "Of course, you'll stay with me as my maid, Abbie. Daniel wouldn't want us to be separated." There was real warmth in her look toward the little serving maid.

"Besides, I could always get a job," Abbie volunteered. "I'm used to hard work."

"That won't be necessary." Betty relented and smiled. "You can cook until I learn how!" An instant later a frown replaced the smile. "Abbie, Mr. Spencer mustn't know we don't have any money."

"No, ma'am." Abbie started to add something but refrained, and Betty leaned her head back against the plush seat, eyes narrowed, mind scheming.

While the train carried them west, Abbie relaxed and enjoyed the changing countryside, leaving Betty to do the planning. Betty was not interested in the changing countryside. She only wished it would change faster. When Abbie roused her to look at something of particular interest her only reply was, "Yes, Abbie, it's nice," before she drifted back into anticipation of Daniel Spencer's face when she stepped from the train. Never once did she take into consideration that he might not be there. She was so caught up in her own dreams that she had no thought but that Daniel would be there with arms outstretched to welcome her.

Daniel was not there when they pulled in.

Haughtily, Betty descended. She had primped as well as the limited means on the train permitted, even changing into her best silk dress. She surveyed the other passengers on the last lap into Pioneer with satisfaction, ignoring their gasps at the daring garb she wore and rejoicing that not one of them could equal her magnificence. Now she stepped from the train — and sank into icy slush over her boot tops!

Her eyes darkened with rage. "Why hasn't

this been cleared away?" Only Abbie paid any attention to her, quickly stepping forward to help her onto the platform. She might as well not have existed for all the notice the residents of Pioneer paid her.

"Sir!" Her imperious command to the tall, good-looking man near the depot door brought him around to face her.

"You were speaking to me?" The almost amused tone set flags flying in her already overheated face.

"Will you be so kind as to tell me how to find Daniel Spencer?"

Was the stupid lout so void of understanding that he could only stare? "Daniel Spencer?" He sounded like a parrot she had once seen.

"Yes. Daniel Spencer." She stamped an increasingly cold foot. "I am Elizabeth Courtland, his fiancee."

From somewhere behind her Abbie gasped, but Betty stood her ground. She *was* Daniel's fiancee; he just did not know it yet.

"I — see." The stranger surveyed her coldly, then turned to Abbie, his face warming a bit toward the shivering girl. "And this is — ?"

"My maid, Abbie Tucker." Betty stamped her foot again. "Really, Mr. Whoever-you-are, it is inexcusable keeping us standing here in this cold. Where is Daniel Spencer?"

In answer, he swung wide the door to the depot, letting out a blast of warm air from the pot-bellied stove. "Step inside, please, Miss Courtland, Miss Tucker."

Betty marched in, closely followed by a frightened Abbie. The quick glance the depot agent shot her was not lost. Betty drew herself up even taller and turned to the stranger closing the door. "Will you be so kind as to inform me where Daniel Spencer might be found? Or would you take a message and let him know I am here?" She fumbled in her pocket and removed some coins, holding them out.

"Your money isn't needed, Miss Courtland." The stranger's manner matched her own for haughtiness as he stepped back, face sternly set against her. "I am Dr. Stewart, Daniel Spencer's best friend. Dan isn't here."

"Not here!" Betty's stare equaled the depot agent's.

"No." Dr. Stewart warmed his hands by the stove. "He is about fifteen miles up the river on a call to an Indian family."

Betty sank weakly to the hard wooden bench nearby. Up the river! "Then Abbie and I will just have to get back on the train and go where he is." She rose, some of her assurance returning.

"Ha, ha!" She whirled, furious with the braying of the station agent, getting even angrier at the impossible situation. Was that hick *daring* to laugh at her?

A glimmer of pure devilry shone in Dr. Stewart's eyes. "Sorry, Miss Courtland. The train doesn't run up the river."

"Then how did Daniel get there?"

"By canoe."

Betty shuddered. "Canoe! You mean one of those dreadful dugout boats?"

"Not dreadful if you're used to them."

"Where can we find one?"

Every trace of laughter vanished. "You can't go to the Indian village, Miss Courtland." Dr. Stewart's glance was even. "I'll take you and Miss Tucker to Dan's cabin. You can stay there until he gets back. He shouldn't be gone more than a day or two."

Betty was silenced. She watched the husky doctor shoulder her suitcase and Abbie's. "Maybe you can get Andy to haul the trunk over," he told the agent. His eyes swept the array of bags and boxes. "And the rest of the stuff." Contemptuously he opened the door for them.

If Betty lived to be a hundred she would never forget that first walk in Pioneer. She stumbled after the long and easy stride of Gordon Stewart, biting her lips to keep from calling out for him to come back and help her. Her feet were frozen. Her long skirts dragged in the slush no matter how she tried to hold them up. By the time they left the town behind and entered the clearing in the trees she was almost numb. She could hear Abbie panting behind her and was thankful when the doctor set down the suitcases and opened the rough door.

"Come in." A match flared, there was the pungent smell of kerosene, and Betty took her first look around Daniel Spencer's home.

All the pride Daniel had put into his little cabin, all the work the good ladies of Pioneer had done went unnoticed. Betty's sophisticated gaze dismissed the cheap curtains, scrubbed hard wood floor, and handmade spread on the big bed. Her gaze riveted on the open fireplace, ashes long dead in it. Nothing mattered now except to warm herself.

"Build a fire, Abbie," she directed, but the doctor forestalled her.

"I'll do it. Miss Tucker can get out dry garments for you both."

Betty opened her mouth to protest, but he was already kneeling by the fireplace, shaving kindling into long curls, setting them ablaze, then feeding chips and sticks, finally banking it all with a great log.

"Get into dry clothes," he ordered. "I'll be back soon."

They needed no urging. The blazing fire had taken the chill from the cabin. By the time the doctor knocked at the door again, both girls were bundled up in the warmest clothing they had brought and were toasting in front of the fire.

Betty was amazed when Dr. Stewart entered with a basket. From it he took rough bowls, heavy iron spoons, and crude knives. He lifted the cloth and set bread on the small table by the fire with a pat of butter. Finally he took out a heavy black kettle and set it in the fireplace, carefully hanging it on the big hook over the flames.

"Hot stew. Cooled off some while I brought it from the hotel."

Betty started to thank him, but he had already turned to Abbie. "Miss Tucker, do you think you can cook over an open fire?"

"I think so." Some of her freckles were covered by the blush from the dancing flames.

"Good. It's too cold for you to want to go to the hotel tonight." He casually inspected the cupboard. "Plenty of cereal for tomorrow. There's a bottle of milk just outside the door in the snow. It's fresh. You can get along all right for breakfast." He glanced at his watch. "I have office hours in a few moments. I'll see you tomorrow."

"Mr. — Dr. Stewart?" Betty hesitated.

"Yes?"

"Where are — where is — how do we — ?"

Dawning comprehension filled his eyes with laughter. "Plenty of water to wash in. Pump's right outside the door. You'll see it's well-wrapped against the cold, so it won't freeze up." He motioned toward a bucket. "Hang the bucket on the crane in the fireplace to heat." From behind the curtain into the alcove he drew out a huge washtub. "Portable bathtub."

"What about the — *facilities?*"

"Outhouse is about a hundred yards down the trail." Ignoring Betty's shocked look he opened the door. "Good luck." They could hear his merry whistle as he walked away.

"Well!" Betty stared at Abbie. "Did you ever see the like? 'Outhouse is about a hundred yards down the trail,'" she mimmicked. "Ridiculous. Didn't these people ever hear of indoor plumbing?"

Abbie's eyes were round, but she skillfully grabbed a heavy towel and removed the now-bubbling stew pot from the stove. "Maybe that's why they call it Pioneer."

It was the final touch needed to set Betty off. She laughed until she thought she would have hysterics, rocking back and forth, clutching Abbie to keep her balance. When she finally subsided, she sank back in her chair. "At least we can eat."

"It smells good too." Abbie dished out the steaming stew. "I'm sorry Mr. Daniel isn't here, but at least we have a place to stay. What if we hadn't met Dr. Stewart? We don't have any money for the hotel."

Abbie's practical assessment of their situation dampened Betty's mirth. "I know. But as soon as Daniel comes back we'll be married, and everything will be all right." Betty began eating the rich stew. "Abbie, at least I have you! What would have happened if you hadn't come with me?" She finished her supper and sat back while Abbie removed the dishes, then jumped up with flushed face.

"Starting right now I'm going to learn everything. You can show me how to do the dishes, cook, and pump water. I have to learn."

"But, Miss Betty," Abbie exclaimed in horror, "you'll ruin your pretty hands."

Betty's mind was set. "Pretty hands aren't

the most important thing in the world, Abbie. Now teach me!"

By the time the dishes were washed and the girls had brought in enough water for both to bathe, they were exhausted. Neither had slept enough on the long train trip. Now Betty curled under the despised homemade coverlet gratefully. Every bone in her body ached. Was that what it meant to be a minister's wife? She could hear the soft, even breathing where Abbie lay asleep in the alcove. Gradually her own eyes closed.

"What was that?"

Through the night air came a horrible screeching sound, bringing Betty bolt upright in bed, Abbie flying to her mistress' side. *S-c-r-e-e-e-e-c-h!*

"Oh, Miss Betty!" Abbie landed on the big bed and was hauled under the covers by Betty. "What is it?"

"I d-d-don't know," Betty said through chattering teeth. "D-did we bolt the door?"

"Yes." Abbie burrowed deeper. "There's a big wooden latch that drops down. Nothing can get in." She crept closer to Betty who put her arms around her while waves of fear threatened to swamp her.

For a long time they lay tense, maid and mistress, clutched in a mutually encouraging grip. At last some of the tension began to leave. Betty's voice was muffled by the covers, against Abbie's shoulder. "Abbie — maybe we shouldn't have come." Her heart raced in the long silence.

"There isn't anything we can do about it now. We're here." The practical Abbie curled into a ball and dropped off to sleep. But long after her grip loosened, Betty lay wide-eyed in the darkness. Yes, they were there, and there wasn't anything they could do about it now. If only Daniel Spencer would hurry home from up the river with the Indians.

9

Elizabeth Courtland woke to a new world. Strangely enough, she felt rested; it must be late. Her faithful watch said nine o'clock, but how dark it was — and how cold. Grateful for the warmth of the still-sleeping Abbie, Betty closed her eyes again. She would wait until Abbie woke up and built a fire before she got up.

The next moment she reversed her decision and carefully slipped from bed without disturbing Abbie. If she planned to be a minister's wife in this horrible place, even until she could persuade Daniel to leave, she had to show him she could make it. Her feet cringed from the icy floor, and her fingers were nearly numb before she could pull on heavy stockings and walk to the blackened fireplace. Perhaps there would be a few coals left to get her started.

There were no coals. The ashes lay gray and dead. Betty swallowed hard and caught up the big knife Dr. Stewart had left by the pile of kindling. Even her warm wrapper did not hold off the chill of the room. With unaccustomed fingers she hacked away at the soft cedar, managing to make a few shavings. Gently she put them in the fireplace and struck a match. They flared. Overjoyed by her success Betty watched them burn, then frantically realized she should have added chips. By the time she gathered the chips her small flame had gone out.

Her second try was more successful. Forcing her freezing hands to carefully add chips a few at a time, then a stick of wood, she felt a thrill. She had actually built a fire! She waited only to see that the stick was catching, then put on more wood as she had seen the doctor do. When it blazed up, she crept back across the cabin and into bed, cuddling against Abbie, her thoughts busy.

Daniel would be home today, or at the latest, tomorrow. The icy apprehension of the night before melted in that thought and in the gradually warming room. He would come, she would tell him about her father, and they would be married. She closed her eyes. Married to Daniel! A flush touched her pale cheeks. With a man like that, even the primitive conditions could be endured until she could change them.

Abbie stirred, opened sleep-filled eyes. "Why, Miss Betty!"

Betty laughed, seeing the puzzled look as Abbie glanced around, then realized where she was. "No more Miss Betty, Abbie, just Betty Courtland, then Mrs. Daniel Spencer."

"Why," Abbie's wondering gaze fell on the crackling fire, "there's a fire. Did Dr. Stewart come?"

"No, Abbie. I built it myself."

Abbie sat bolt upright in bed. "You!"

Betty flushed under the innocent criticism, and her chin lifted. "Yes, I. From now on I learn to do everything there is to do."

Abbie flopped weakly back on her pillow. "But, Miss Betty, I mean, Betty, I meant to —"

"I know you did, Abbie." Betty sobered. "But you must let me learn; you must teach me. I have to show Daniel Spencer I can fit into his world before I can take him back to ours."

Abbie was speechless, but Betty hopped from bed. "Let's get up. I'm starving. Didn't he say something about cereal in the cupboard? Besides," she made a face, "I'm going to have to take that hundred-yard walk."

Abbie could not have moved if her life had depended on it. She watched as Betty determinedly slid into layers of petticoats, struggled into her dress, and backed up to the bed to be buttoned, then slipped through the door. She was not gone long.

"Of all the inconvenient — !" Her hands were red from the cold. "Honestly, Abbie, that outhouse is the coldest place I've ever been." She sighed. "Well, there isn't any other choice, but just wait until you've been out there!"

Abbie finally came alive and hopped out of bed. It only took moments for her to slip into her warm undergarments and the dark gray dress she usually wore to work. She glanced anxiously at Betty's silk. "Miss — Betty, don't you want to wear something else? I don't know how things get washed out here, but if you get that dress dirty we might have a terrible time getting it cleaned."

Betty looked down at the fancy dress and back at Abbie. "I suppose you're right. I just wanted to look nice when Daniel came, but —" Her eyes roamed the cabin and lit on a large towel. "I can put that around me. Besides, until the other baggage comes, I don't have any other choice."

Somehow between them they managed a creditable breakfast. Abbie found the cereal and cooked it in the hanging black kettle. Betty discovered a long handled fork Abbie told her was for toasting bread, and after dropping the first two pieces in the ashes and flames, she managed to turn out two more that were only burned slightly.

"It isn't quite like breakfast at home, is it?"

"No." Abbie turned her head to hide her pity, thinking of Betty propped up at home against lacy pillows with a breakfast of hot rolls, freshly squeezed orange juice, a puffy omelet, and perhaps sausage on a tray before her.

"But that's all right." Betty was determined not to think back. "I knew it wouldn't all be easy."

Before they quite finished breakfast a knock was heard. Dr. Stewart stepped inside, a slight smile thawing the frozen look Betty associated with him. "Well! I see you're all set up. Miss Tucker, you evidently know how to adapt to circumstances. That's a good looking fire, and I see you made breakfast."

Betty was suddenly, hotly angry. "I'll have you know *I* made that fire, Dr. Stewart, *and* toasted the bread!"

The smile she hated flashed. "Amazing. Congratulations, Miss Courtland. I wouldn't have suspected it."

Leaving her tongue-tied with rage, he turned to Abbie. "Miss Tucker, I wonder if you would like a job?"

"A — a job?" Abbie faltered, glancing across at Betty.

"Yes. You look like a sensible girl, and I need someone to help me in the hospital. Ever done any nursing?"

"Just taking care of Miss — of Betty when she was sick."

"You're strong and can learn. I'll teach you what you need to know. It will involve staying with patients when they are in the hospital and needing care I don't have time to give. What do you say?"

Abbie glanced back at Betty helplessly, an appeal in her eyes. Betty thought rapidly, seeing recognition in Abbie's eyes of their dwindling funds. There might not be too many chances for work here. Everyone probably took care of their own work.

"If you want to, Abbie, go ahead." To stress her complete indifference she added, "I can take care of everything here while you're gone, especially until Daniel gets back."

Dr. Stewart's bland innocence did not deceive her. Betty ground her teeth as he said, "Oh, of course. Anyone who can toast and build a fire should have no trouble with other household chores."

Abbie's voice was small. "If you think I can do it, Dr. Stewart, I'll try."

"Good girl!" His look was warm and approving. "If you don't mind, I could use you right now." He bowed elaborately to Betty. "That is, if Miss Courtland doesn't mind."

"Not at all." She managed to rise with some of her natural haughtiness, even to smile. "It is the neighborly thing to do. Isn't that the word they use out here, Mr. — sorry — *Dr.* Stewart?"

For just an instant she was rewarded by admiration in his eyes, but he merely turned to Abbie. "We'll go then. Good morning, Miss Courtland." With another bow he opened the door for a half-frightened Abbie to scuttle through and then added, "Have a pleasant day."

Betty stared at the door closing behind him, torn by an impulse to call Abbie back. How could she spend the entire day in this isolated cabin? Yet after she was married to Daniel wouldn't she be spending many such days, especially if Abbie continued her work with Dr. Stewart? Soberly she collected the dishes they had used for breakfast and stacked them. Abbie had thoughtfully filled the big bucket with fresh water and hung it on the crane. She tested it for hotness in the small tin dishpan she found, valiantly struggled with the pump until she had a pan of cold water to temper it, and washed the dishes, drying them carefully and putting them away.

The fire was dying, and she dared not let the room chill. Hastily she rebuilt it, this time carrying a huge log to roll in behind the flames. Sparks flew, and she beat them out.

"Oh, no!" There were holes in the white towel she still wore for an apron. What if she had not put it on? Her best dress would have been ruined. Her hands were sooty and her hair coming undone by the time she got the fire well banked.

"Elizabeth Courtland, Daniel Spencer was right. You really aren't good for much," she told herself as she passed a small square of looking glass. Her image grimaced. "Well, I can learn. I'll show that man — *and* Dr. Stewart, if it's the last thing I do!"

A quick partial bath restored some of her spirit. Emma had said she could learn, if she wanted to learn badly enough. She surveyed the cabin. What should she do next?

"The bed. It needs to be made." Some of the quilts were on the floor from where she and Abbie had huddled against the night noises. "Get up there, you," she threw the quilts in a heap, then tried to smooth them, ending up by taking the whole thing apart. Finally, red-faced and gasping, she managed to get everything in fairly neat order.

Even the top coverlet quilt was smooth. Again she felt that little thrill that had come when she built the fire. She had never given any thought to satisfaction that comes from work well done.

"I guess there are just a lot of things I've never thought about!" She dropped to a rude chair by the fire and stared into it. "Everything's just always been done. I never noticed how much there was to do." Now her eyes spied crumbs under the table and litter on the hearth. A worn broom stood in the corner, and Betty attacked the floor with vigor. Moments later she was coughing at the dust she had stirred up. Gradually she slowed her strokes until they caught up the offending dirt but did not raise dust. She swept it directly into the fireplace.

"Well, Abbie should be home soon. It must be late," she peered outside into the gloom. A few snowflakes had begun lazily drifting down. She glanced at her watch. Twelve o'clock. Had it stopped? It must be later than noon! She shook it. No, it was ticking steadily. Disheartened she dropped back into her chair. What did people *do* in this country when all the work was done?

"I do believe I'm hungry again." She foraged the cupboards, but everything was packaged or needed to be cooked except one slice of leftover bread and a little milk in the jar. She toasted the bread and drank the milk. It would have to do. But what about dinner? Dr. Stewart would bring Abbie home and wonder why she had not started any dinner preparations.

For a moment she toyed with the idea of going to the hotel for a hot meal but decided against it. There was so little money left it might not cover their meal, and if Daniel were delayed — she firmly shoved the thought aside. She had boasted that she could handle things in the cabin; now she had to make good.

In the cupboard she found a package of rice. Good! She loved it. If she cooked rice, they could have something hot. There were glass jars of fruit. Had someone given them to Daniel? She peered at the neat rows, wondering why there was so little. Did Daniel eat at the hotel instead of cooking? He must or there would be more provisions. Well, once she learned to cook that could stop.

There were no instructions with the rice, but she knew it must take water to cook, so she confidently put a small amount in the hanging black kettle over the fire and added some rice. It did not look like very much. Maybe she should add more. They could re-heat it for the next day. She put in the rest of the package and stirred it. Funny, it did not look like enough water now. She added a dipperful, reluctant to have to struggle with the pump out in the cold for more.

"It still doesn't look like much. Maybe I'd better fill up the kettle." By the time she got back in with skirts wet again and dumped in water to the top of the kettle she was out of sorts. "Why would anyone in his right mind choose to live in this place? Daniel did not have to come. He chose to come." She grimly rotated in front of the fire, drying her bedraggled skirts.

"Miss Courtland," a hail from outside brought her to the door. Could Daniel be home? It was only the station agent with a strange kind of sled affair. Face beaming, he pulled the sled to the tiny porch of the cabin. "Brought your duds."

Betty rather resented his familiarity but forced a smile. "Thank you. Bring them in here," then. "Please." She must remember she was not at home where one ordered servants about.

The agent was panting and puffing by the time he took in all the bags, boxes, and the huge trunk. Betty had directed him to put them all in the little alcove. The spare room seemed to be a study of sorts. For now, they could stay in Abbie's cubicle.

"Right cozy little place here, ain't it?" the beaming man eyed the cabin, making Betty glad she had cleaned it. "Nothing like what it was before the preacher came. All the womenfolk jumped in and made curtains and gave him the bedding and stuff."

Betty looked around with new eyes. Then the furnishings had been gifts. They took on a little more importance. "That was kind."

"I hear tell you're going to be his woman."

For one awful moment Betty thought she would have hysterics. That red-faced man calling her Daniel's "woman" seemed the height of impertinence. Elizabeth Courtland — to be Daniel Spencer's "woman"!

Her silence did not daunt the friendly agent. "Pioneer's a whole lot better place since he came, him and the doc. Soon's the town gits wind you're here, they'll be coming to call." He held out his hand, and she reluctantly shook it.

"Welcome to Pioneer, Mrs. Minister."

Betty's hand still felt the warmth of the hearty shake as he closed the door behind him. Some of the warmth stole into her troubled heart. Mrs. Minister! The ignorant man could have no way of knowing what the words meant to her. They had succeeded more in reconciling her to her surroundings than anything else could have done.

Betty forced herself to survey the cabin, seeing it again through newly awakened eyes. It was not more than crude logs, yet they were chinked against the cold. The panes in the little window were shining clean. Those cheap curtains, evidently made from friendship for "the preacher," were crisp and clean. She moved to the bed, fingering the quilt, noticing for the first time the tiny, tiny stitches. Someone had made that quilt, setting those stitches one at a time — and giving it to Daniel, in love.

I don't belong here. The shattering truth rocked Betty until she felt physically ill.

"I don't belong here!" she cried out to the open rafters, the fireplace with its now bubbling burden, the cupboard with curtain in front of it. "I can never fit in. I don't know anything!"

Depression grayer than the outdoor gloom swept through her and in desperation she threw herself on the newly made bed, fighting tears until from sheer nervous exhaustion she slept.

Daniel Spencer was tired. The trip to the Indian village had been one of sadness. The chief's son was sick. Gordon Stewart had confided, "There's no cure. Too far gone before I came — consumption."

So Daniel had made the long trip to give what comfort he could. The impassive brown faces did not hide the chief's sorrow or that of his family. The dark eyes steadily watched Daniel as he talked with the child, tried to make him understand that the "happy hunting ground" was even more beautiful than the world he would shortly leave. In the time Daniel had been in Pioneer he had learned to blend the language of his own faith with the vocabulary of the Indians rather than impose strange new terms. Now he spoke to the child about Jesus, the "Great Spirit's Son," who had come to earth to die that children such as Bright Arrow might go to be with Him.

The canoe trip back down the river was silent until they beached just outside of Pioneer.

"Daniel Spencer, when Bright Arrow dies, you will say the words?"

Daniel gripped the chief's hand. "When Bright Arrow dies, you bring him here. I will say the words."

He stood for a long while watching the chief turn the canoe and paddle back up against the current, going with him in spirit, entering the rude abode, waiting for the end.

If only they had come sooner! If he and

Gordon Stewart had been in Pioneer even months earlier, Bright Arrow could have been saved.

Dog tired, discouraged, he started for his cabin. At the edge of the trail toward the little hospital he hesitated. Should he go see Gordon for a time? No, it was office hours. He would go home, rest from the sleepless night of the trip, and see his friend later.

The snowflakes that had lazily descended earlier had grown in intensity, turning hard, stinging his eyes. He walked rapidly, glad to be back. There was nothing worse than feeling totally helpless to do anything. At low ebb, now all he wanted was to get home, and the little log cabin had become a real home.

He increased his stride, visualizing the warm fire he would build and the sleep he would get before going to the hotel for dinner. No, maybe he would eat whatever was on hand instead of going out again.

Just a few more yards now. His cabin loomed up. The sense of smell heightened by his months in pure air stopped him in his tracks. Something was cooking. His mouth stretched in a grin. Gordon must have suspected he would be back tonight and come over to fix dinner. Funny, there was no light in the cabin.

He dropped his pack on the tiny porch floor with a thud and pushed open the door, sniffing again. Something was burning and badly. From the light of the open fire he could see his kettle with lid raised off by something white boiling over and over into the coals below. He snatched an old towel and seized the steaming mess. Rice? Why would Gordon — ?

From behind him, in the shadowy corner of the room where his bed was came a gasp. Dropping the sticky kettle to the hearth Daniel whirled toward the sound.

"Who are you and what are you doing in my cabin?"

He struck a match — and gazed directly into the frightened face of Elizabeth Courtland.

10

"Daniel!" It came out as little more than a whisper. Relief flooded away her fear. Daniel had come home; everything would be all right. She could see his fingers tremble as he lit the kerosene lamp, then held it high, still disbelieving what he saw. "Madcap Betty? What is this, another of your stunts?"

She was cut to the quick. For him she had given up everything, only to have him speak in that harsh voice. Where was the loving welcome she had dreamed of ever since leaving Grand Rapids? Disappointment choked off any self-defense she might have made. Even in the pale yellow lamp-light she could see how Daniel had changed. He was no well-dressed city visitor. Before her stood a man whose shadow loomed behind him on the rough walls, perfectly at home in those awful surroundings. Gone were city clothes, replaced by a dark blue shirt open at the neck and dark blue pants. Yet even as she tried to adjust to his strangeness, something within her cried out to be in his arms.

Daniel's words fell like hard little stones, bruising her already shattered composure.

"I've seen a lot of bold stunts but never anything to match this. Just what do you think you're doing?" He marched to the alcove, contemptuously looked at the trunk, bags, and boxes. "What made you think you could come out here and move into my cabin while I was gone?"

Betty bit her lip, stripped of pretense. "I — I — Prescott told me —"

"Prescott told you what?" His voice was granite overlaid with lead. There was not a trace of weakening.

Betty licked her lips, finding words hard to get out. "He said you cared —"

She was not prepared for his harsh laugh. "With what right did he tell you such a thing? I left no message for you but goodbye."

It was too much for Betty. She hurled herself against the wall between them. "How can you, a professed man of God, speak to me like this?"

"It is because I am a man of God that I must."

Hope died. He would never believe that it was more than one of her stunts. For one moment Betty passionately regretted the name she had built for herself. Madcap Betty! Well, if he thought it of her she might as well live up to it.

"You don't think you can stay here, do you?"

It was her turn to laugh, although her lips had gone white. "I could if I were your wife." She saw the effects of her taunt, the involuntary step he took toward her before thrusting his hands into his pockets. She laughed again, noting the brittleness of the sound in the otherwise quiet room. "I built a fire this morning. I toasted bread, swept your floor, and made your bed. I put rice on for dinner —" Her eyes fell to the ghastly mess on the hearth. She was silenced. A drift of white disaster mutely bore evidence of her failure.

Daniel's face was no longer pale. Dark color and a beating pulse in his throat shone in the dim light. With one stride he caught her by the shoulders and swung her off the bed and to her feet. "And you think that is what it means to be a wife? Don't push me, Elizabeth Courtland! Why did you really come out here?"

For a moment Betty thought she would sink through the floor. A great leap of hope spurted. "Because of what Prescott said." She faced him steadily, conscious of the gripping fingers that would leave bruises as their mark. "And because — I —" she threw her head back defiantly, "I care."

"I don't believe you."

She wrenched free, rage tumbling out almost faster than she could speak. "I don't care if you believe me or not. I couldn't stay in Grand Rapids. My father has never stopped believing the worst of me. I brought Abbie, and we came here thinking you would take care of us." Was there an imperceptible lessening of the strain in his face? Betty dropped her eyelashes and played her last card, swaying toward him. "I found out life wasn't worth anything without you, Daniel." Every wile of her coquettish youth shone in her confession.

"Even if it was true, which I doubt, it wouldn't matter."

Betty stared. How could he stand there, arms folded? Why had he not taken her into his arms?

"You don't think I'm sincere, or don't you think I'm good enough for your royal palace?" She gestured around the sparsely furnished cabin.

"No, Betty Courtland, you aren't. My God is head of this household. He always will be. I don't think you'd find it comfortable living here with me — or with Him."

The infinite sadness touched her more than all his anger had done. Betty reeled backward and would have fallen if the bed had not caught her. "I — see."

A poignant light came into Daniel's face. "Betty, can you honestly say you could marry me and live here under those conditions?"

Betty's mind raced, her heart rejoicing. He cared! He must care to look like that! And yet — live with the shadow of his God over them? She shuddered.

Daniel's lips tightened; the light in his eyes went out. His voice was colorless as he turned away. "I'll arrange for your baggage to be moved to the hotel, Miss Courtland. You mentioned Abbie was with you?"

"Yes." A stranger had taken over her voice. It could not be she answering in that calm way. "Dr. Stewart gave her a job." Mustering the shreds of her dignity Betty stood. "Thank you for sending my baggage." She stumbled blindly toward the door. She was arrested halfway.

"Betty." Was there pleading in his voice? Another moment and she would fling herself into his arms, beg him to marry her regardless of that God of his. One more step to freedom — she took it, stepped outside into the snow, and ran. The mark of his tracks showed the way. Pounding steps behind her increased her speed. Soon he was up with her, turning her around, laying her cloak across her shoulders. In the last dimness with snow falling around them his eyes looked like black coals in a white blanket. "You can run away from me, Betty, but you can never outrun God."

She clutched the cloak and ran again, only pausing when she came to the rude board hotel. It would not do to appear breathless before those inside. What would they think if they knew their precious minister had practically thrown her out? Her lips curled. Why think of him? She would stay overnight at the hotel and go back to Grand Rapids in the morning.

No! A little moan escaped her lips. She could not go back to Grand Rapids. There was barely enough money to pay for her dinner. She would have to ask Daniel for money.

"Never!" She set her white teeth into her lower lip until she could taste the sickish taste of blood. "I'll starve first!" Yet as she paced the cold porch of the unfriendly hotel hopelessness overcame her. What could she do except ask him? She could write Prescott for money, but it would take time to get it. Her father was out as a possibility. Would Gordon Stewart lend her train fare? She could not ask. He was Daniel's friend and would report straight to Daniel.

She had to get the money, at least enough to get by until she could write Prescott. Through the windows she could see tables of men seated before steaming platters of food. Memory of her sketchy meals made her mouth water as the tantalizing dinner odors crept through the cracks. Her eyes narrowed. There had to be a way.

"I'll do it!" Suiting action to thought she entered the hotel door, taking a deep breath.

Instant silence fell as every eye turned toward her, the same silence that used to greet her entrance back home at a social event. It did wonders for her bruised ego. She lifted her chin, put on her most charming smile, and crossed the room to the man in the white apron who appeared to be the proprietor.

"Something I can do for you, miss?" He took another keen look at her. "Say, ain't you the preacher's gal?"

She fought down an impulse to walk out and only smiled again. "I am Elizabeth Courtland. I would like a room, please, and dinner."

"Of course." He beamed at her. "Will Mr. Spencer be joining you?"

"Not tonight." She dropped her eyes demurely. "He just got in from up the river and all."

"That's fine." The proprietor elaborately led her to a small table a little way from the others, giving her a feeling of privacy. "We call it supper out here instead of dinner, miss. I'll send one of the gals."

"Thank you, Mr. —"

"Just Buck. We ain't much for misterin' out here." He was warming under her smiles just the way she had hoped.

Betty decided it was the strategic moment to strike. "Buck, I'm wondering if you would give me a job waiting tables."

"You?" If the horrified look on his face were an indication, she was in for a battle.

Betty lowered her voice and leaned forward mysteriously. "I hope you can keep a confidence."

He perked up immediately. "I shore can."

"You see," Betty began, "I've always wanted to write a book about a place like Pioneer."

"A book? You mean about folks like us?"

"Yes." Her eyes glowed. "Back East people really don't know anything about the kind of men who open up the wilderness and make it safe for women and children. They think it's all rough and wild." Good heavens, could he possibly swallow that?

Betty stifled a nervous giggle and lowered her voice even more. "It's a surprise, even for Mr. Spencer. My friend Abbie is working for Dr. Stewart now." She had had to substitute "friend" for "maid." "I thought if I could wait tables it would give me the chance to get to know a lot of Pioneer residents." She flashed her famous smile again. "But I have to confess, Buck, I don't know much about waiting tables."

"Why, that's all right, Miss Courtland," he gave her a conspiratorial wink and a fatherly pat on the arm. "You can learn."

Betty had one more trick. It *had* to work! She risked everything. "Of course, since I'm new and all, I wouldn't expect to be paid. It's to give me experience and get me acquainted."

He fell for it even better than she hoped. "That wouldn't be right at all!" His genial face took on an unaccustomed scowl. "If you work, you'll be paid the same as the other girls. Board and room and —" The paltry sum he mentioned almost brought a gasp of indignation. Just in time Betty remembered her part and smiled brilliantly.

"I insist, Miss Courtland." He swept over her with a glance, and the worried look returned. "Just one thing —"

"What's that?" *If hearts can stop, mine will,* Betty thought. *Everything has gone so well.*

What can hold it up now? I have to have the job!

"The other gals are all called by their first names." Buck looked doubtful. "And your clothes — ain't you got anything not quite so fancy?"

Betty's heart bounded. "I'll expect to be called Elizabeth, of course." She hid an inward shudder at the thought of those crude loggers calling her that. At least she would not have the humiliation of them calling her Betty. "And when my trunk is unpacked I have other clothes. I don't have any aprons, though."

"We have aprons." The beam came back to his face. "Does Mr. Spencer know what yore aimin' to do?"

"Sh!" Betty twinkled her eyes and placed her fingers over her lips. "I'll take care of him."

"Ha, ha!" Buck's laugh drew every eye in the room. "Well, I'll send supper, and you can start tomorrow. Four-thirty."

"You mean I don't work until afternoon?"

"I can see you have a sense of humor, Miss — Elizabeth. We start servin' breakfast at four-thirty so the loggers can get out in the woods."

Once more Betty stifled a gasp and shudder. "It's going to be quite an experience." But when he had gone it was all she could do to get down the tasty supper. In order to be ready for work at four-thirty in the morning, what ungodly time would she have to rise?

Somehow she managed to finish a meal and stumble up the stairs behind Buck.

"You said you had a friend, Abbie? You want two rooms?"

"Of course —" But Betty hesitated. Two rooms would cost twice as much. She was getting hers free, but if Abbie took one it would have to be paid for. The quicker they got the money for passage together the faster they could get out of this terrible place. She went on smoothly, as if she had not thought rapidly. "— No, we can share."

"Right in here." He held the lamp high. The room was small, barely big enough for two iron beds, a chest of drawers, and hooks on the wall covered by a curtain serving as a closet door. At least it was clean.

"It's very — clean." Betty could not do better than that.

"You bet. Our maids keep this place clean. I'll get you a pitcher and bowl." He set down the lamp. "Want I should bring your friend Abbie up when she comes?"

"How will you know her?"

His tobacco-stained lips split in a grin.

"When you live in Pioneer, you know out-siders. 'Sides, Doc'll probably bring her over." He looked around the room again. "If you need anything else, just holler."

The door closed behind him, leaving Betty alone in the strange room that would now be home. Compared to the cozy cabin she had left earlier, it was nothing. So bare. Yet what did it matter? She and Abbie would be gone soon. How many weeks would it take with their two salaries combined to pay fare home?

Homesickness overwhelmed her. Even her father's sternness melted a little in the face of the terrible longing for home. If only she could be free, waiting for Prescott to come to take her to a dance or a luncheon. Why hadn't she been satisfied with what she had instead of chasing after a man who did not want her? Outsiders, Buck had said. He was right. She and Abbie *were* outsiders. She fought a rising hysteria. Should she "holler" the way he told her to if she wanted any-thing? What she wanted was to be safe back in Grand Rapids where she could forget anyone named Daniel Spencer existed.

"Miss — Betty!" Abbie's eyes were round with shock as she interrupted Betty's misery.

Betty noticed Buck in the background

and hurriedly drew Abbie in, talking to cover what she might blurt out. "This is our new room, Abbie. You can have the bed by the window. I've already unpacked what we'll need for tonight." She forced a smile to the waiting proprietor. "Thanks, Buck. See you in the morning."

"G'night." He was gone, mercifully leaving Betty and Abbie alone.

"But what are you doing here?" Abbie demanded, eyes still popping. "Dr. Stewart took me back to Mr. Spencer's cabin, and he was there, but you weren't!" She looked straight at Betty. "You didn't quarrel, did you!"

"Quarrel!" Betty almost shrieked the word. "It was more like a fight to end all fights."

"Then you aren't getting married?"

"Never! At least not to him."

"Then what're we going to do?" Abbie dropped weakly to her neatly made bed.

"I've got a job waiting tables here. You can keep on with Dr. Stewart. When we get enough money we're going home."

"But, Miss — Betty! Don't you love Mr. Spencer?"

The storm broke. "Yes, I love him! I even thinks he loves me. But we'll never be married. He told me God lived in his house, and

I wouldn't be happy there." Betty's face flamed through the tears. "He's right. I don't even know this God he talks about all the time. Even if I did, I'd never be second to some unseen something. I'm going to work and go back to Grand Rapids, and someday Daniel Spencer will come crawling, begging me to marry him. When he does I'll laugh in his face and tell him to go find that God he thinks so much of."

Abbie gasped, her face reflecting her horror. "That's blasphemy!"

"Is it?" Betty's eyes were great purple orbs. "He told me I couldn't outrun his God. I'll show him. Just wait and see."

Abbie held her tongue, unable to speak in the face of such fury. Finally she suggested, "We'd better go to bed. I have to be up early tomorrow. Dr. Stewart has a man coming in before work and wants me to see how he does dressings."

In spite of her anger and woe Betty caught something in Abbie's voice. "You like what you did today, didn't you, Abbie?"

"Yes." The little maid's eyes glowed. "Dr. Stewart says I have natural ability. Miss — Betty, when we get back to Grand Rapids, if you don't need me, that is, do you think I could learn more about being a nurse? Then when you do get married and have babies I could take care of them when they were sick."

Betty stared. She had never seen Abbie so excited. Her answer came slowly. "Why, I don't see why not." She sighed. "But first we have to get there. At first I thought I'd write Prescott for train fare. Now I think I'll just wait until we can earn it. Then when we leave I can throw in Daniel Spencer's face the fact that we had to go to work in his precious town even to get money to leave!"

"How long do you think it will take?"

Their eyes met. "I'm afraid most of the winter, Abbie. Can you stand it?"

Abbie's eyes were sober. "It won't be me that has trouble standing it, Miss Betty. I'm afraid it's going to be you."

11

Abbie's words proved true. By the end of the first day on her job in Pioneer, Betty Courtland thought she would die. Unaccustomed to any work at all, standing on her feet, carrying heavy platters of food in white hands that had never held anything heavier than Beauty's reins was sheer agony. By the time breakfast was over she was too tired to eat. Buck sent her upstairs for an hour's rest warning, "We get a big dinner crowd."

Dinner? Betty remembered. To her it was lunch. She threw her weary body on the hard bed thankfully and did not rouse until Buck tapped on her door. He sounded apologetic. "Sorry to wake you, Miss Elizabeth, but it's time to set up for the crowd."

Betty hurriedly splashed water from the basin on her face and pasted on the stiff smile she had worn that morning. She managed to get through the meal and help clean up, then stumbled toward her room that had become a haven. It was Abbie's entrance that woke her.

Abbie was full of chatter, perched on her own narrow bed while Betty freshened up.

"I'm learning so much! Dr. Stewart says he couldn't ask for a better helper." Her eyes glowed, then the lamps in them went out. "Oh, he and Mr. Spencer will be in for din— supper tonight."

Betty unconsciously squared her shoulders. The moment she had feared was upon her. Neither Daniel nor Dr. Stewart had appeared at breakfast or the noon meal, although she had started every time the heavy door opened.

"I wonder what he's going to say when he sees you here?" Abbie looked worried.

Betty moistened her lips with the tip of her tongue. "I don't know. It really isn't any of his business, anyway." She finished smoothing her hair and tossed her head with some of the old haughtiness. "The sooner I get it over with, the better."

Abbie followed her down the stairs, scooting into a far corner and watching her former mistress with concerned eyes.

"Hello, Miss Tucker. Ready for a good, hot meal?"

Dr. Stewart's bright greeting spun Abbie back to attention. She smiled back at him. "Oh, yes, Dr. Stewart!"

"Where's your friend? Not down yet?"

Abbie gasped as Dr. Stewart and Daniel Spencer dropped to chairs at her table.

"Why, she's —" The words choked in her throat as Betty crossed the crowded room to their table.

The sound of her voice brought both men to their feet. "May I help you, gentlemen? You wish the full din— supper menu, of course?"

"Betty!" Daniel Spencer's face had gone brick red, then deathly white.

"I am known as Elizabeth during my working hours, Mr. Spencer." She deliberately turned her back on him and smiled at Dr. Stewart. "Will you have coffee now or with your supper?"

"Now, please."

"And you?" She turned back to Daniel, in perfect control of herself, at least outwardly. Inwardly she quivered like the small dish of strawberry jelly she had placed on the table earlier.

Daniel did not answer; he merely stared until Dr. Stewart sat down, pulling Daniel with him. "Bring coffee for all three of us, Elizabeth. That is, if Miss Tucker doesn't mind our having supper with her?"

Abbie was shocked into speech. "No, I don't mind, not at all."

"Very well." Betty sensed a wave of bitterness threatening to engulf her. How things had changed! Out here she was "Elizabeth," her former serving maid was "Miss Tucker." She shrugged impatiently, careful not to let her face show any of her hatred of the situation. Even her hands were steady as she poured the coffee.

"Is this another one of your jokes? Or are you going home tomorrow?" Daniel finally found his voice and demanded in a low tone.

"Home? Oh, you mean to Grand Rapids?" Suddenly her laugh was clear to every corner of the listening room with staring men. "Buck has promised to be patient. I'm going to learn to cook and clean and whatever needs doing. Abbie and I will be staying here in the hotel all winter, at least." There was nothing in her words to give the wide-open ears of the hearers anything to talk about.

"Impossible!"

Again, Dr. Stewart's warning hand kept back further comment. Daniel lapsed into silence as Betty Courtland moved gracefully around the crowded room carrying food, laughing at the sly sallies of some of the loggers. Andy, in particular, seemed charmed by the Eastern girl. Daniel overheard him say, "Ma'am, you don't know how much good the doc 'n' the preacher have done. Glad yore here."

Betty just smiled, conscious of Daniel's eyes following her. She had always been a good actress, taking parts in home plays for friends and the like. Now she used every bit of her amateur skill and grew almost radiant. "Why, thanks. Andy, isn't it?" Her magnificent eyes deepened. "Daniel and I are both thankful you feel that way."

Abbie gaped, and Dr. Stewart stifled a chuckle; but Daniel Spencer rose and stalked through the door, letting it bang behind him. Andy's grin got wider. "Say, he shore was in a hurry. Don't s'pose he's a mite bit jealous, do you?"

Betty stared at Andy, the seed of an idea sprouting. "Why, no." Twin dimples flashed as she confided, "Besides, we aren't married — yet." For one moment the response in the man's eyes frightened her, and she drew back; but he laughed, and she moved on to serve the next man.

"Miss Tucker." Dr. Stewart's stern voice drew Abbie's eyes like a magnet. His face was serious. "Better tell your friend she can't use her Eastern charm out here. It's dangerous to flirt with these Pioneer men. You've probably noticed that we're short of women, especially young, attractive women. These men are simple. If a woman asks to be insulted by her actions, she also lowers herself in their esteem. They don't understand all the modern goings on that Betty Courtland was used to back East."

"Well!" Betty herself stood at their table, coffee pot poised.

Dr. Stewart rose and reached for his hat. "I meant what I said, Miss Courtland." Even in her rage she rejoiced that he had not called her by her first name. "You're lighting a fuse to dynamite if you flirt with these loggers."

Venom sprayed through her until her voice was hoarse, almost undiscernible. "I will act in any way I see fit, Dr. Stewart."

"Not in Pioneer you won't. You're supposed to be the minister's fiancee. As such, you've been given a pedestal. See that you don't fall off." He tipped his hat, more to Abbie than to Betty. "Good night. I'll see you in the morning, Miss Tucker."

"Elizabeth." Buck's call sent Betty scuttling for the kitchen. "Take this extra platter of chicken to the big table, will you?"

It was only the beginning. By the time Saturday night came Betty was too tired to care if she lived or died. How many weeks of it could she stand before she just curled up and expired? The work was hard. The men were courteous but also curious. Every meal at least one asked, "When are you and the preacher gittin' hitched?" She always managed some light answer but inwardly boiled. What right did these oafs have to ask her such personal questions?

Abbie fared better. She was totally absorbed in her new work. She came home nightly with tales of Dr. Stewart's kindness. "He's so gentle, Betty!" The "Miss" had long since been dropped in sharing the same plight and room. "He delivered a baby today, and I've never seen such a look in a man's eyes for a squallin', little red baby."

Betty shuddered. The last thing she needed was to think of squalling babies. She had troubles enough of her own. "Too bad it didn't die. Who'd want to grow up in such a place?"

"Betty!"

"You needn't glare at me, Abbie. I didn't really mean it." She crossed to their bit of a window and looked out. "Did you ever see such desolation?"

"Dr. Stewart says when spring comes it will be beautiful."

"I don't think spring will ever come."

"Tomorrow's Sunday. Are you going to the church service?" Abbie held her breath. Betty was so unpredictable lately that she never knew what to expect.

"I suppose so. Buck said they have meals

at different times 'so's those who want to, kin go to the meetin'.' I almost laughed in his face."

"I really kind of like it here. When you get to know some of the wives and children, it's not so bad —" But Abbie saw Betty was not listening.

The next morning Betty did not admit it, even to herself, but it was good to lay aside the plain garments that she had chosen for work and put on something prettier. She chose a blue dress that matched her eyes at their bluest, with tiny bands of red braid down the front and a row of red buttons to match. She even dug into the bottom of the mostly unpacked trunk for a matching hat with red plumes.

"Oh, Miss." Abbie's shock brought back her former servitude. "Miss Betty, you aren't goin' to wear that to church?"

"And why not?"

Abbie's face turned crimson with embarrassment, but she bravely held up her chin. "I heard one of the women talking about red hats or anything red. Out here it's considered — bad." She brought the last word out reluctantly.

"Bad!" Betty's lip curled. "Of all the backwoods —"

"It's what they think. And you're the minister's fiancee — or at least everyone thinks so."

Without a word Betty ripped the red plumes from the hat, leaving only the blue with a tiny line of red trim. She had already confided to Abbie what she meant to do. "I'll live according to all their traditions, show them what a perfect minister's wife I'll be. Then when I'm gone, he can explain just why I left — if he dares!"

If she meant to shake Daniel by her presence, she failed utterly. He preached as she had heard him preach before, sincerely, from the depths of his heart. Betty pressed her handkerchief to trembling lips to deny the stirrings of her own heart. What if she did believe in his God? What if everything he said was true? Marriage with Daniel Spencer could be a glimpse of the heaven he spoke of, right here on earth.

"Miss Tucker, may I have the honor of walking you to your hotel?" Dr. Stewart stepped forward when church was over.

Abbie shot a frightened glance at Betty, then nodded and took his arm. Betty was left standing alone.

"Waitin' for the minister, huh, Elizabeth?"

She hated the familiarity and almost turned an icy stare at the innocent Andy, who had surprisingly been in church in the little one-room school. Framing for the church was up, but the weather had kept it from being finished.

"Why —" She made up her mind and swept Andy a glorious smile. "Why, yes."

"Here she is, Preacher." Andy turned to Daniel as he stepped out of the building.

"Thanks, Andy." Daniel stepped down and took her arm, leading her gently away from the worst muddy spots in the road. Once away from the loggers' curious eyes he asked, "How long are you going to continue this farce?"

"Farce?"

His jaw was set in the way she had learned to know. "Yes, farce. If there is anything more ridiculous than you working in that hotel I don't know what it could be."

"I consider that my business."

"It's my business because you chased out here after me."

In that moment she hated him. Every indignity she had faced, every humiliation heaped up in a pile to accuse him. "It's all your fault! Why did you ever come to Grand Rapids, anyway?" Regardless of any watching eyes she jerked free and faced him, stamping her foot on the muddy road. "Do you think I like being here? Do you think I'd stay if there were any other way —" She broke off, appalled at how close she had come to giving her penniless state away.

"Any other way to get what you selfishly wanted." He had misunderstood her completely. "You are still the same spoiled child I knew in Grand Rapids. I hoped, once you were here, you might see the value of these hard-working people who are trying to carve out homes."

Betty's unruly heart leaped. He could not speak so to her if he did not still care.

"I fail to see why anything I do should interest you at all. Good day, Mr. Spencer." She turned, caught the hem of her skirt on a partially hidden boulder and would have gone down if he had not snatched her.

"I will walk you to the hotel. No use advertising to the whole town just how things stand between us."

"I am no more eager to advertise than you." She spoke no more until he opened the hotel door for her. "Thank you for walking me home, Daniel." The added sweetness was for the benefit of anyone who might be listening.

"My pleasure, I am sure." Daniel's farewell left Betty seething. It was the last time she would go to church. Let Pioneer make of that what it would.

But when the next Sunday came Betty could not face the four walls of her own room in her hours off duty. Even sitting through the torture of Daniel's sermon, aching to be at peace, was better than brooding in the little room that was not even all hers. There was not even privacy to cry if she wanted to do so. Abbie worked long, hard hours and needed her sleep. Betty did not realize her consideration of Abbie was something that had grown since coming West. She only knew Abbie needed rest. She herself was usually so tired from working she fell asleep the moment her head touched the uncomfortable pillow.

And then the snows came — not little flakes, but great, soft winter whirlings that left the ground blanketed with beauty. Even Betty's spirits rose. The world was clean. The defects of Pioneer were covered with that mantle of freshness. That night sleigh bells rang outside the hotel. Dr. Stewart bounded in. "Miss Tucker, Miss Courtland, we're having a sledding party. Will you come?"

Refusal trembled on Betty's lips. She was tired. She had had to help cook that evening and burned one hand painfully in the process of lifting bread from the oven.

"Could we, Betty?" The longing in

Abbie's face decided her.

"Go ahead, Abbie."

"Not without you," faithful Abbie pleaded. "You need to be out."

"Yes, Miss Courtland." Dr. Stewart's keen eyes seemed to see right through her. "The fresh air will be good for you."

"Is Mr. Spencer — Daniel going?"

"No. He's tied up."

Betty's heart bounced again. Why not? She dropped her eyelashes as she used to do when she was belle of the ball back home. "That's too bad. Well, maybe I'll go anyway."

"Good! Put on your oldest, warmest things."

Fifteen minutes later the girls were bundled into the big sleigh along with about a dozen more laughing young people. Betty looked around her astonished. "Why, where did you all come from?"

The shout of laughter warmed her heart. "Most of us are home from school," a girl near told her. "Sue and Abigail and Tom and James and I all go to Normal School, and we're home for the holidays." She counted off on her fingers. "The others are either friends or relatives who have come to spend Christmas with us."

"Christmas!" Betty's shocked repetition

196

was lost in the general uproar. She had lost track of time. What would it be like to spend Christmas in Pioneer? For one moment she felt nauseated, remembering the beautiful home she had left, the gigantic Christmas tree with dozens of tiny tapers. Sam and Abbie had always been near with buckets of water in case the flames touched the branches. She drew in a quick breath of the clear, cold air. Would she ever spend Christmas in her own home again?

The evening went by in a blur. All Betty could remember afterward was the beauty of the night and the feeling of security being tucked in between others of her own age. Problems seemed suspended as the group shouted songs, laughed, and finally ended up at a farmhouse for steaming oyster stew. It was the best thing she had eaten since she arrived in Pioneer. When she was working the food odors took the edge off her appetite, and she had lost a tremendous amount of weight. Now she ate as if she were starving, never noticing the relief in Dr. Stewart's eyes.

"Your friend seems happier tonight," he whispered to Abbie later.

"I'm glad." The little maid turned her trusting, freckled face toward him. "It hasn't been easy for her."

"And you?"

"I love my work. It makes all the difference, you know."

Dr. Stewart's eyes widened as he looked into Abbie's upturned face. "Yes, it does." His gloved hand felt for her little mittened one under the blanket that covered them both. "Abbie." It was the first time he had called her that. "You'll never know how much it means to me for you to be working here."

"Thank you, Dr. Stewart." But the shy glance from blue, blue eyes held more than appreciation.

Betty had missed the whispers but looked up in time to see Abbie's face. Stupefied, she could only stare. Abbie, looking like that? And Dr. Stewart — he actually looked human. But before she could digest what she had seen they were at the old farm. Light streamed through the welcoming door.

"Why, I thought we were going home!"

"Not us," Dr. Stewart told her, eyes shining. "This is another family who have kindly provided dessert for us." He helped both girls down. "Can't you smell that peach cobbler?"

Again Betty ate until she could hold no

more. The peach cobbler had been topped with heaps of thick whipped cream, billowing over the edges like the snow drifts they had seen on the way out.

"Too bad Daniel couldn't be with us," Dr. Stewart remarked casually, his eyes intent on Betty's face.

"Yes, isn't it?" Betty's eyes challenged his in the moonlight now highlighting every white, burdened branch. "But then, if I'm to be a country minister's wife, I suppose I have to get used to it."

Dr. Stewart was still for a long moment, then said, "Yes, if you are to be a country minister's wife, you will have to do just that."

Was there the slightest emphasis on the word *if?* Betty turned to the girl closely packed on her other side with a bright remark about what fun this was, but inside her heart thumped with fear. Just how much did Dr. Stewart know about her?

Suddenly the joy of the unexpected evening fled, leaving Betty more alone than ever before, especially when she saw Gordon Stewart turn to Abbie with the same warm look of approval she had intercepted earlier.

12

It was Christmas Eve. Work at the hotel was over. Most of the men were home with their families or anxious to get through and ready for the "big doin's" at the schoolhouse.

Betty did not know when she had ever been so tired. Her lips trembled as she hung up the last dish towel. One of the other girls had been sick, and Betty helped clean up. Dejectedly she made her way upstairs.

"Oh, Betty," Abbie's eyes were like two stars in her highly freckled face. "Hurry! We don't want to be late for the program."

"I don't see how you can get so excited about a hick town Christmas program." Betty bit off the rest of her complaint. The faraway look in Abbie's face told her Abbie was not even listening.

"Abbie, you've grown positively pretty since we came here."

"Do you really think so?" Abbie took a step nearer, peering into Betty's face.

"Yes, I do. You look happy." Betty could not keep the unconscious envy from her voice. "Funny. I was the one who was going to find everything I ever wanted in Pioneer, but it's you who is happy."

Abbie fell to her knees by Betty's bed, both hands taking Betty's sadly disfigured ones in her own. "Miss Betty, I am happy. I wasn't going to tell you, but —" Her face suffused with color. "Dr. Stewart — Gordon — has asked me to marry him." She faltered before Betty's shocked expression.

"And you —"

Abbie's eyes were wells of happiness. "Do you remember so long ago when you asked if I'd ever been in love?"

"Only too well." Betty took in a deep breath, trying to smother her pain.

"I told you no. I can't say that any longer." Her face grew serious. "From the first time I saw him I knew I loved Gordon Stewart."

"Are you sure, Abbie? It's not just because you work with him and he's a kind man?"

"No. When he told me about the girl he loved who died I knew he'd never love anyone else. I was wrong. He has learned to love me."

"But if you marry him you may have to spend the rest of your life in this hole!"

"It isn't a hole to me. Not when Gordon is here." Abbie rose and crossed to the window, looking into the black night with courage in her eyes, a slight smile on her lips.

"You'd really stay here forever, just because of Dr. Stewart?" Betty was horrified. "Or will you try and get him to go back to civilization once you're married?"

Abbie whirled from the window. "Oh, no! This is our home."

Betty fought the urge to throw herself on the bed and cry her heart out. Even Abbie had betrayed her.

"I've been thinking, Betty." Abbie was back at her side. "With the money we've both saved, you'll have enough to go home right after the New Year. I won't need mine. You can have it."

Betty's lips quivered at the generosity of the other girl. "You'll need it, Abbie. You'll want sheets and pillowcases and everything to set up housekeeping."

"No, Dr. Stewart already has enough. I want you to take the money. Your papa and mama will forgive you if you tell them you're sorry. You can marry Mr. Prescott. He will give you everything you ever wanted."

"Except the man I still love."

Two strong arms crept around her. "Oh, Betty! You mean you still love Daniel Spencer — after all this time?"

Betty flinched from the pity in Abbie's voice but bravely lifted her chin. "I can't help it, Abbie. It won't do any good. I've worked and tried to hate him, but I can't. If only I could be his wife!"

"Would you be content to stay here in Pioneer?"

One lone tear escaped the tightly shut lashes. "I don't know. I only know that when I go back to Grand Rapids it will be slamming the door on something that could have been very precious. If it hadn't been for his God, things would have been different."

"I wonder."

Betty's eyes popped open, anger rising. "Just what is that supposed to mean?"

Abbie's gaze was steady, unafraid. "I mean if he had been just like everyone else, all the other young men in Grand Rapids, you wouldn't have cared any more for him than you did for them. The reason you fell in love was not in spite of Daniel Spencer's God but because of Him!"

"That's not true." Betty flounced to the mirror, watching Abbie's dim reflection instead of her own. Abbie did not budge an inch, even when Betty stubbornly repeated, "It's just not true."

"Isn't it?" Abbie gathered her cloak, tied her bonnet strings. "What do you think makes him different? It's his belief, his partnership with God." Her face softened at the misery in Betty's image. "Come on. Go with

me to the program. You'll like it. I understand there's something on the tree for everyone in town."

Betty sniffed. "I suppose that was Daniel's ridiculous idea."

"It isn't ridiculous. It's a time when the
whole town can join together for a little
while and enjoy each other." Abbie hesitated in the open door. "Aren't you coming
at all?"

"No."

"Then, good night, Betty. Merry
Christmas." The little figure that had suddenly acquired a new dignity disappeared
from sight. Betty could hear her light steps
running down the stairs to meet Dr.
Stewart. In spite of herself she crossed the
room and looked down through her little
window. Dr. Stewart had tucked Abbie's
arm through his own. The flaring light from
his old lantern shone for a moment on their
laughing faces, sending another pang
through Betty. What if Daniel should look at
her like that?

Hot tears stored up through all the long,
hard working hours threatened to flood
Betty's eyes. She held them back and frantically fumbled in her trunk for a dress. She
would go to the program after all. It could
not be worse than sitting alone in this

prisonlike room, envying Abbie with all her heart.

Betty slipped into the last available chair in the back corner when she got to the church. It had begun snowing again, and she gladly relinquished her cloak with its heavy hood to a smiling man she recognized as the depot agent. Curiously she surveyed the packed building. Abbie had been right — everyone in town must be there! What if she really were the minister's wife, part of the watching crowd? For the first time she saw them as individuals, not just loggers and wives, store owner, doctor, or teacher. She caught the kindly approval in glances sent her way, and her heart beat wildly. What if they knew it was all a hoax and she would be leaving as soon as she got the fare? Would that kindly regard change to stern disapproval?

Something stirred, born of Abbie's news and the fact that it was Christmas Eve. Maybe it would not be so bad living in Pioneer with Daniel after all.

She turned back toward the little platform built from a few hastily thrown together planks. A large Christmas tree stood near. The children were intent on presenting the Christmas pageant. Betty craned her neck to see around the burly shoulders of the man in front of her.

"I'm sorry. There is no room in the inn." The youthful innkeeper looked down his nose at the miniature Mary and Joseph.

Betty winked back tears, furious at herself. What was wrong with her? So she had never been to a Christmas Eve program before. She had danced Christmas Eve away at balls and parties. Must she make a fool of herself? Still she found herself listening intently.

"I have a stable. You can go there." The innkeeper gestured, and Mary and Joseph turned away.

In wonder Betty watched the rest of the pageant, unable to withdraw her gaze. What a lot of work! Every child knew his or her part perfectly. The background scenes had been painstakingly formed. Had Daniel done it all? She could have helped. She often painted for her own pleasure when she was growing up.

Then it was over. The little group around the manger with the shepherds who had come to worship and the look of love Mary gave to the real baby in her arms lent reality to the scene. Daniel Spencer stepped to the side of the group. He looked thin and tired in the glow of the candles on the tree, but exalted. Betty's heart gave one leap, then settled back in dullness.

"I'm not going to preach tonight. In a few moments we will distribute the Christmas gifts — something for everyone. I just want to ask one question. You have seen our children portray the search by Mary and Joseph to find room for the Christ Child. My challenge to you this Christmas season is: Will you find room in your heart for the Christ Child? He is still looking for a place to abide. Or, like the innkeeper, will you turn Him away? If you do, you can know He goes sadly. Once more, is there room in your heart for God's Son?"

Betty could not stand any more. A wild impulse to rise and cry out, "I will make room" was stopped only by action. Stumbling over knees in the semidarkness she got to the door, snatching her cloak from the agent who held it out to her. She had to get away. Was that then the secret of Daniel Spencer's success — a personal magnetism that hypnotized people into accepting his God? Almost hysterical, Betty ran through the snow-covered town back toward the hotel. At least she would have privacy. It would be a long time until the Christmas tree was dismantled of its gifts and Abbie returned.

There was no peace in her room. The light showed her distraught face. The darkness held Daniel Spencer's accusing eyes. Had they looked directly at her? Or was that God looking at her from the corners of her room?

"God, if You really are, what have You to do with me?"

For what seemed hours she paced the floor, finally sinking to her bed in sheer exhaustion, only to be roused by Abbie.

"Betty?" A wave of cold air from Abbie's garments brought her back to reality. "I thought I saw you at the program."

It took all of her control to answer carelessly, "Oh, I dropped in for part of it."

Abbie's concern showed with the hastily struck match and the yellow glow of their little lamp. "You didn't stay to receive your present. Mr. Spencer asked me to bring it." She stooped to pick up something from the floor by the doorway and crossed to Betty's bed. "These are for you."

Betty was speechless. Red roses, a whole dozen of them. She hadn't seen roses since she left Grand Rapids. "But how — who —"

"There's a card."

Betty held the card in her hand and silently read it in the dim light.

MERRY CHRISTMAS, ELIZABETH.
Daniel

The tears would no longer be denied. Betty cradled the roses to her breast, tears softly falling to the heart of the beautiful flowers.

"He must have had them sent in on the train," Abbie told her, eyes still wide. "Betty, he must love you a great deal to do this."

Long after Abbie slept, Betty stared into the darkness. One of the red roses caressed her cheek, its soft petal and gentle fragrance reminding her of the sender. Some of the storm of the early part of the evening had passed. But just before sleep finally claimed her, Elizabeth Courtland, proud and haughty Eastern beauty, whispered, "What shall I do? Oh, what shall I do?"

It was several days before Betty saw Daniel again. Through Abbie she learned that he had gone to the Indian village to spend time with the people he had learned to love. That time she did not shudder. It all fit what she had learned of him since she came to Pioneer.

Then one night he was at the table with Abbie and Dr. Stewart.

"Good evening, Miss Courtland."

Betty's heart sank beneath the long white apron protecting her dress from her work. She had hoped the roses would soften the hostility between them. She had no way of knowing the fight Daniel experienced within during his trip to the Indian village, or that he had seen and correctly interpreted her turmoil the night of the program.

Now she merely answered, "Good evening, Mr. Spencer. I'll bring coffee right away," and turned from him without meeting his eyes. When she returned it was to hear him say, "Gordon, I wish you'd go to the Indian village with me tomorrow. Some of the children seem to have a red rash. Looks like it could be measles." His brow wrinkled. "You know how hard these diseases are among the Indian people. They don't have any immunity to it. Strange thing, though, it's only on their stomachs."

Gordon's keen eyes flashed. "Is it small red spots? Are you sure they don't appear on arms and legs?"

"I'm sure." Daniel leaned toward his friend who had turned pale. "What is it? Something other than measles?"

Gordon glanced at Abbie and Betty, openly staring at him, and clamped his lips shut. "I can't say. We'll leave early in the morning." He finished his meal in silence.

"What do you think he suspects?" Betty whispered to Abbie after the two men were gone.

"I don't know." Abbie's face was solemn.

"But it doesn't sound very good, does it?"

The next night Abbie rushed in, wild-eyed. Seizing Betty's hand she managed to draw her aside from her work. "Don't tell anyone, but there's typhoid fever in the Indian village." Betty gasped, but Abbie rushed on. "Dr. Stewart came back as soon as he discovered what it was. Half the village is sick and many of the others have symptoms. Dr. Stewart and Mr. Spencer will stay with the Indian people and take care of them." Her hands were like ice. "I wanted to go with them, but they wouldn't let me."

"Well, I should hope not." Betty was indignant.

"You don't understand! They could get it and die."

Only Abbie's quick clutch saved Betty from falling. "You mean —"

Abbie could not hold back the truth. "After Dr. Stewart was gone I read everything I could find in his medical books about typhoid fever. It comes from drinking impure water and is passed on by flies. Betty, Mr. Spencer was bound to have drunk the same water the Indian people drank while he was up there."

"What can we do?" Sheer terror lay in Betty's face.

"Wait — and pray."

Abbie had predicted well. All Pioneer waited and prayed. The only ones who visited the Indian village were the doctor and the Indians who brought him down by canoe for supplies and waited at the river. Abbie carried on at the hospital, valiantly doing her best, assisted by those loggers with rudimentary knowledge of first aid. Betty continued her work, no longer aware of the long hours. In her state of numbness she could only wait. She tried to pray but did not know how, except to sometimes whisper, "Help him."

News from the Indian village was not encouraging. Many of those who contracted the disease died. Others were weak, still needing care. January slipped into February without notice. Every time the doctor came for supplies he looked grimmer. Then one day Abbie came home with different news.

Betty was sitting in their little room, staring blankly at the wall when Abbie came in. "What is it?"

Abbie's thin face, worn with work and worry, looked sick. "You know they found the source of the impure water some time ago." She paused, and Betty's nerves screamed.

"Well, Dr. Stewart thinks the village is over the fever." She turned away, her voice muffled. "He came home today — with Mr. Spencer."

"Is he — ?"

Abbie flung herself into Betty's arms. "He's sicker than any of the others. Dr. Stewart said he had to get him back here for there to be any chance at all." Tears were running freely. "He was so run down taking care of others —"

Something snapped inside Betty. "He's not going to die?"

"I don't know." Abbie's reply was a wail. "Dr. Stewart said it would take a miracle to save him."

"Then that's what he's going to have." Betty snatched her cloak and started for the door.

"Where are you going?"

"I'm going to take care of him. Tell Buck, will you? He will understand."

"But Betty, you can't!" Abbie jumped up in horror. "Gordon won't let you into that cabin. He said no one in Pioneer except himself can go in. I'm to leave supplies at the edge of the clearing, the way I did while he was at the Indian village. He won't take any chance of sickness spreading through Pioneer."

Betty's pale, determined face did not waver. "I won't spread it. I'm going to that

213

cabin, and once I'm inside, nothing on earth will get me out of it." She swallowed fiercely. "I may not know anything about Daniel Spencer's God, but I know this — if there really is a God like Daniel believes, He's not going to let Daniel die. I'm going to be right there to see to it!"

She yanked open the door and turned back to Abbie. "If you ever prayed, Abbie Tucker, you'd better pray now. I'm not good in that department, but let me tell you — Daniel Spencer is going to get well, and when he does, I'm going to marry him no matter what it costs. If I have to live in Pioneer the rest of my life and learn to serve the God he worships, I'll do it. There's nothing or no one, including Daniel himself, who can change that."

The door slammed behind her. But the white-faced little maid huddled on her knees by the side of a hard bed scarcely heard. She had been ordered to pray; it was all she could do. Daniel Spencer's God would have to do the rest. As Dr. Stewart had said, nothing could save their minister except a miracle.

13

"What are you doing in this cabin?" Dr. Stewart's iron grip and fierce whispered demand nearly undid all her determination.

Betty raised her pale face and jerked away, panting from the run through the snow from the hotel to the little log cabin in the small cleared area. Disheveled, breathless, she managed to get out, "I'm here and I'm staying. If you try and put me out I'll scream until every person in Pioneer comes running to see what's happening!"

The doctor's red-rimmed eyes from lack of sleep burned into her very soul. "Another act, Miss High and Mighty?"

She caught the lapels of his rough coat and peered into the now bearded face. "This is not an act. I have to be here with Daniel."

Something in her pleading face snapped the bonds of Dr. Stewart's better judgment. "Can you take orders?"

"I can."

"Then get out of that wet cloak. There's work to be done."

Daniel Spencer's gaunt face was etched

forever on Betty's heart as she entered the sick room where he lay. Burning with fever, unconscious of her presence, he tossed and turned constantly, arms reaching out. Mumbled and incoherent sentences escaped his parched lips.

For one moment she hesitated. Dr. Stewart spoke in a low tone. "Are you sure you want to be here?"

"I *have* to be here."

He was convinced. "Then do as I say." He rolled up his sleeves and motioned for her to do the same. "He didn't let me know how far advanced his symptoms were, and I was so busy I didn't notice. It wasn't until the last case in the Indian village was on the mend that he said, 'Gordon, old man, we'd better get home. I think we're in for some rough weather.' "

"You love him, don't you?"

"Like a brother." He shot her a keen glance under bushy brows. "And you?"

"With all my heart."

"Then why —" he cut himself short. "I have no right to ask that."

"It's all right." Betty was glad to be able to talk it out with this man whose skill would give Daniel the finest earthly attention possible. In whispered voices, hands busily bathing and sponging the feverish, tossing man they both loved, she told Dr. Stewart, "I was intrigued at first, then furious at how useless he thought I was. Later I knew he was the only man for me. I broke my engagement to Prescott, Daniel's friend. My father thought I was — was unworthy of the Courtland name. Perhaps I was. Not through anything I had done wrong, but by my demand for admiration. Then I came to Pioneer."

Dr. Stewart's hands slowed, then stilled. He wiped them on a towel and motioned her into the other room. His eyes never left her face as she spoke.

"I hated it, all of it." Apology shone in her dark blue eyes, along with honesty. "I think I hated you too. You were his friend. I was — nothing." She took in a deep breath, staring into the fireplace where she had once built a fire and cooked rice until it ran over the edge of the pot to the coals below.

"Why didn't you leave and go back to Grand Rapids?"

Betty forced herself to meet his eyes. "I almost did. My parents wouldn't have helped me, but I know Prescott would have sent money for train fare." A faint smile hovered on her pale lips. "I imagine you're glad I didn't go and take Abbie."

She did not wait for a reply. "Daniel

doesn't know it, but I am penniless until spring and my inheritance comes. Abbie and I had most of our money stolen on the way here."

Dawning realization touched Dr. Stewart's face. "You mean — then working at the hotel wasn't to humiliate Dan? You really needed the money?"

"Yes. At first I was just going to work until I got money from Prescott. But I never wrote Prescott for money. I decided to earn it myself. I had to prove I could."

"To Dan?" His voice was gentle.

"I think more to myself." Again her eyes met his squarely. "You know, he was right. Before I came here I couldn't do anything except paint or embroider or play the piano." She looked at the work-roughened hands. "I'm proud of the way they look now. These hands know how to cook and wait tables and do dishes and sweep. They show it. If my friends in Grand Rapids could see them they would shudder with horror — just as I would have done last fall."

"Why didn't you tell Dan the truth?" Dr. Stewart's piercing gaze saw through her, demanding an answer.

"I couldn't. He told me the night he first came home from the Indian village how things stood. I even told him I loved him, wanted to marry him."

"And?" The word cracked like a rifle.

Betty met his question head on. "He said God lived in this cabin, and I would never be happy here in His presence."

Dr. Stewart grunted. "What did you say?"

If it had been possible for Betty's face to turn even whiter, it would have done so. Yet she had determined to bare her soul. "I told Daniel nothing. I shuddered — and ran away."

In one stride he was at her side. "You did that, to a man like Daniel Spencer, a proud man who has fought his own feelings for you all these months, trying to follow the God he serves?"

"Yes." All the condemnation of that same God fell on Betty's defenseless shoulders. Then with some of her old fire she cried, "What else could I do? I don't know his God."

"Have you ever tried?" A tiny pulse beat in Dr. Stewart's forehead. "I didn't know God either, until I came here with Dan. In the months we've worked together I've learned that God is just what Dan says — loving." He turned away from the fire, hiding his face for a moment. "When the girl I loved died, I hated God — if there was a God. I, a doctor, couldn't save the one I loved! Then I met Dan. I still don't know why God let her die. I do know that I've found peace and contentment — and Abbie. I know Dan's God allowed everything to happen as it did. He didn't make Susan die. But neither does He want me to spend my whole life mourning.

"As I've walked this clean land, breathed in air free from the grime of cities, seen snow cover the harshness, I look forward to spring and rebirth. I know *I've* been reborn, Elizabeth. I am not the same man who came to Pioneer only a few short months ago. Abbie is not the same woman; neither are you." He cleared his throat, then finished gruffly, this time facing her, "Only Dan is the same. The reason why is that he brought faith in Christ with him. The rest of us had to find it here."

Something akin to hopelessness touched Betty, sending a cold breath across her body. "But I haven't found Him."

"You will." For the first time since trying to throw Betty out of the cabin Dr. Stewart smiled.

"I — I tried, a little. I tried to pray when I knew you had gone to the Indian village. Then on Christmas Eve — the manger scene, I felt —" Betty helplessly threw her hands wide. "Does Daniel Spencer hypnotize people into believing in something that doesn't exist? Or if God does exist, why does Daniel feel He's interested in individuals?"

"I asked myself that question a hundred times, Elizabeth. Now I feel like Dan; I can only believe God is and cares. Why things happen as they do is not for me to know, at least not at this time." Infinite sadness touched his face. "I don't know why God would allow Dan, of all people, to be stricken with typhoid fever. I can only do my best and let that same God take care of the rest."

A low moan from the other room snapped them back to their duties. Daniel's fever had risen again, in spite of the cooling sponge bath.

All night long, the next day, and the next night Dr. Stewart and Betty took turns watching and bathing Daniel. There was no improvement. If anything, the fever rose higher, his cries became more incoherent. His emaciated form seemed scarcely alive. His cracked lips uttered meaningless sounds and the once strong hands now picked at the coverlet.

Betty grew thinner, whiter, unable to eat even when Dr. Stewart forced food on her. Daniel worsened. If he died, everything on earth would stop for her. Was this God's punishment for her making war against Him? She voiced the question to Gordon but she was only partially satisfied when he shook his head and said, "God is not vindictive or small, Betty. He loves us so much He sent His only Son, that whoever believes on Him might not perish, but have everlasting life. Surely you have heard Dan preach that."

"It didn't mean anything," she confessed, eyes gigantic in her peaked face. "I was too busy hating God for taking Daniel."

"And now?"

"God could never forgive me." There was hopelessness in her voice.

"When you know you are a sinner and ask Jesus to forgive you and live in your heart, you have that forgiveness." He looked at her sternly. "But you can't just make a sham and think it will save Daniel's life. The transaction has to be between you and God, and it has to be real."

Betty's head drooped as Dr. Stewart slipped into the other room. She was so tired of fighting. Her idea of making God the object of her selfishness had been insane. Was it true what Gordon had told her? Could forgiveness really be that simple? There was no problem in admitting she was a sinner. Neither was there a problem in knowing Jesus must have been waiting a long time for her to acknowledge Him.

"Is there room in your heart for God's Son?" Daniel's challenge at the Christmas Eve service struck her with the force of a blow.

What had she done? Even while she had fought tears at the thought of Mary and Joseph's being turned from the inn of old, she had steadfastly refused to admit that same Jesus was seeking room in her life.

With shock Betty realized that neither her position nor her wealth could make her acceptable to the God she had chosen to battle. A conviction began to grow. Daniel was right. So was Gordon Stewart. Her head reeled.

Before she could think it all out or even more than recognize something wild and sweet that came with the knowledge, Gordon returned. His face was haggard. "I don't know why he isn't dead." Unashamed tears stood in his eyes. "I can do no more. I've prayed and given the best care of which I am capable. Still he's dying."

Betty gave a terrible cry of protest, automatically snatched up her cloak, and flung wide the door, answering Dr. Stewart's curt, "Where are you going?" with, "I am going to find God — and His Son."

"Betty, come back —" The closing door cut off his cry.

Betty struggled for footing in the fresh snow, her brain on fire. Where should she look for God? She had to find Him, tell Him there was room in her heart for His Son. She had to tell Him she was a sinner and ask for forgiveness. She had to let Him know that no matter what happened with Daniel, she could fight no more. She was His — for keeps.

Would even God's great love cover the deliberate way she had acted? Were her sins too great for forgiveness? No, Dr. Stewart had said God's love was so great He allowed His only Son to be crucified to save the world from even such sins as hers.

Now her only question was — where could she find God to tell Him, to confess what she had done, and to claim the promise of forgiveness and salvation through Jesus. How strange that those phrases came to mind! Or was it? She had heard them many times, especially since coming to Pioneer. Even while she had ignored any application to her own life they must have been working into her heart and soul.

The church! She had felt God there on

Christmas Eve. Her faltering footsteps started down the way she thought was back to town. Then she remembered. She could not go there. She was a possible carrier of the dread typhoid.

The hotel, where she had felt the same on Christmas Eve? No. Abbie and the others must not be exposed.

"Where are you, God?"

The mocking wind caught her words, whirled them away, ate them alive before they had gone a foot from her lips.

A great fear entered her. Now that she knew the truth, what if she could not find God to tell Him? Yet God was a God of love. He would not hide Himself from her cries.

Like a wraith from the past words from months before flickered in Betty's mind. Dan's voice, urging her on, giving strength. Reverent and deep and sincere. "My God is head of this household. He always will be."

With a cry of joy Betty struggled to her feet from where she had fallen heavily a few moments before. Why, of course! Why had she run into the storm in search of God? He was there all the time! Why hadn't she known it sooner?

If God was in the cabin, He was also in the storm. He was there right now beside her.

He was everywhere. All she had to do was tell Him.

Elizabeth Courtland, proud society belle, dropped to her knees. The icy wind was unheeded as she bowed her head. "I'm sorry, God. I wanted my own way. I wanted it so much I would have done anything to get it. Forgive me. I am sorry for everything. Most of all for not making room in my heart for your Son, Jesus."

She hesitated and one tear escaped the tightly closed lashes to tremble on her face then drop to the ground and freeze. "I'm not even sure I can understand how much love You had to send Your only Son to die — for me. I thought I loved Daniel more than the greatest love on earth, but it's nothing compared to Your love. I accept that love and the gift of Jesus. I know now Jesus is the only One Who can save me, and I thank You for sending Him."

Something deep inside Betty melted, something she hadn't known was frozen. The single tear gave way to others, but they were not tears of sadness now.

With a start, Betty came back to the present. Her cloak had fallen back and while she still felt warm inside, her hands and face were freezing. She peered through the ever-deepening gloom. Which way was the cabin?

She hastened to the left and plunged into untrodden snow. She turned back to find herself caught in hanging underbrush, fighting snow-laden branches that had suddenly become a trap. Abbie had told her never to be out in a storm. People who had become lost were later found frozen to death within a few hundred yards of Pioneer.

"I will not die out here!" Determination gave her strength. "I have so much more to live for now." She tore at the brush, worked through — only to find herself facing a large unfamiliar tree. She fought back through the thicket and the branches that gleefully held her as her own.

Finally Betty could go no farther. "I'll stop and rest for just a moment." She sank onto a big log. The storm lulled her into closing her eyes. If only she could sleep for a few minutes! With tremendous effort she opened her eyes. "No, I mustn't. If I go to sleep I'll die."

She struggled back to her feet, still talking to herself. "It doesn't seem so bad now. If I die, I'm forgiven. I'll see Daniel again."

A spark flared. "Coward!" She came back to full consciousness. "God expects you to do your best. Now that you know Him, you must tell others, just as Daniel did." Faces from Grand Rapids formed in the little thicket ahead: Prescott, her parents, others. "God, if Daniel lives, we can work together. I need him. If he doesn't make it —" she set her teeth in her lip, hard "— I'll go on and do what I can."

She paused. "But, oh, if I could just tell him I've truly accepted Jesus before he dies!" Her foot hit a hidden root and it threw her. Snow surrounded Betty, was in her mouth, up her sleeves, under her long skirts.

Was that God's eye looking at her? She focused on the bobbing movement. "I'm here, God."

Strong arms picked her up. It was Dr. Stewart.

"Where's God?" she asked stupidly. "I saw His eye looking at me."

Dr. Stewart sounded funny. "You saw the lantern." He picked it up with difficulty and helped her back to the cabin, taking great steps through the snow.

"God was there. He's everywhere. So is Jesus. I did what you said. I told Him how wicked I had been. I told Him I didn't see how He could still love me but that I knew He did. I told Him I wanted His Son, Jesus, as my Savior and asked Him into my heart."

Even in the dim light of the lantern she

could see Dr. Stewart's face light up. His arms tightened about her. "Thank God!" Another few strides and they were inside the cabin. Betty stripped off her wet cloak and ran to the fire.

"Betty." Dr. Stewart's voice stopped her. "It wasn't a bargain for Daniel's life?"

She spun around. "No, Gordon. Once I left this cabin I didn't think of Daniel except as someone from my past. The only important thing was to be forgiven."

There was humility in his face as well as gladness. "Forgive me. I had no right to ask."

"You had every right." She looked toward the bedroom. There were no moans now. "No matter what happens, I found out tonight that Jesus Christ is the most important thing in life. Nothing else matters." She quietly slipped into the little room.

Dan lay as she had last seen him, eyes closed, pale as death. This time instead of reaching for a soft cloth, Betty clasped his hands between her own. She must reach the man who had traveled so far toward the fine line between life and death it seemed impossible for him to be snatched back.

"It's Elizabeth, Dan. I'm here." Her voice was clear, but there was absolutely no response.

"I just want you to know I accepted the Lord Jesus Christ into my heart and life tonight. I've been forgiven for everything, even fighting against God. I also want you to know that if He takes you, I think I'll stay in Pioneer, at least for a time. Did you know Abbie and Gordon are getting married? I don't have any money until spring, but when I do we can have the church you wanted. If you can't be here, we'll try and find another minister." Her lips quivered as Dr. Stewart quietly came in.

"Is it all right to keep talking?"

"Go ahead." The slump of his body told her it didn't really matter.

"You said God is head of your household. I know now He isn't a far-off something, but Jesus Christ, alive and living in His followers."

On and on she talked, often rambling. At last Dr. Stewart motioned her away. Before she went she bent low. "Good-bye, my darling." She drew away, repelled by the chill of his lips, to stand before the fire once more.

Betty looked around the rude cabin. She belonged — now. If Daniel died, perhaps she could buy it and spend her life here where she had met her Lord.

Dr. Stewart's hand fell on Betty's shoulder. The timbre of his voice sent a surge of feeling through her. "There is a slight change. The crisis is past. He is sleeping naturally."

Color filled her face. "You mean there's a chance?"

"A slim one. One in a thousand. Sometimes there is a final rallying before death. Other times the patient recovers after much care. He is in God's hands."

The words that would have struck Betty dumb with terror a few days before now sent a burst of hope through her. "We will pray."

The long way back was an uphill fight. There were times when the death shadow hovered close, but as the last storm of winter ended, Daniel Spencer crept slowly back to life. He was strangely apathetic, even when blue sky could be seen outside the window and an apologetic sun sent feeble rays to earth.

Dan did not yet know Betty cared for him, or even that she had been there. He did not ask about her, and Dr. Stewart let her stay with him only while he slept.

"I'm afraid of his reaction." He turned away from the hurt in her eyes. "He doesn't know how you've changed."

Days later Dan stopped his friend as he prepared to leave the bedroom. "Say, old man, isn't anyone else sick in Pioneer?

Seems you're here taking care of me. What about the others?"

"Oh, I've had some help." Gordon tried to sound disinterested.

A flicker of interest crossed Dan's face. "Abbie still here? I thought she and Miss Courtland would be gone by now."

"Not yet."

Dan looked puzzled.

In the other room Betty crept nearer the doorway, trying to hear above the thudding of her heart. "I thought they were going when spring came?"

"Abbie isn't going at all. We're getting married as soon as you're able to do the job." Gordon grinned at his patient.

"Well! Good for you. She's a fine girl. Miss Courtland is staying for the wedding, I suppose. That's nice of her."

To the eavesdropper just outside the doorway his apparent lack of interest cut deep. From her vantage point she could see Dr. Stewart's eyes narrow as he dropped back into a chair. "You don't know just how good Miss Courtland has been, Dan. She's been here helping me the whole time you've been sick."

Dan raised himself on an elbow. "Here? Madcap Betty's been playing nursemaid to me?"

Gordon's sober face helped restore that same nurse's composure. "I thank God she was and is Madcap Betty! She came here the night I brought you from the Indian village, as soon as she heard you were sick."

"And you let her stay?" Dan sounded incredulous.

"I had no choice. She forced her way in and threatened to scream her head off if I threw her out."

It sounded to Betty as if the doctor was enjoying himself.

"She cooked and cared for you. She followed orders like a soldier. She lost weight and couldn't eat. Still she stuck."

Dan was staring. "Betty Courtland did all that for me?"

"It isn't all she did." Gordon went into a brief description of the hours of desperation they had shared and then added in a quiet voice, "I finally had to tell her you were dying. I could do no more."

The ticking of the old clock sounded like a cannon in Betty's ears.

"What did she say?"

If Betty had doubted interest, his question told her those doubts were unworthy. His eyes blazed darker than she had ever before seen them.

"She looked at me and gave a cry that was

almost inhuman. She ran for the door. It was the worst storm of the winter. I asked where she was going —" Dr. Stewart stopped for breath.

"What did she say?"

"She said" — Gordon's voice was almost reverent — "she said, 'I am going to find God — and His Son.' " He seemed to anticipate the next question hovering on Dan's lips. "I had told her earlier how God loved her so much He sent His Son to die in her place. I also told her she couldn't pretend in order to save your life.

"I called for her to come back. She ignored me. I had to check on you again, but when she had been gone a long time, too long, I knew I must go to her. She was not far away. She was turned around." Gordon drew a ragged breath. "When she saw my lantern she thought it was God. She wasn't scared. She had confessed herself a sinner and accepted the Lord Jesus Christ out in that storm, just as Abbie and I did not long ago.

"I listened at the doorway when she told you about it, wanting somehow for her words to pierce your unconsciousness. She also told me other things, Dan. Betty stayed in Pioneer because she had no money to do anything else and was too proud to ask for help. She also stayed to prove she could be worth something. Daniel Spencer, if I didn't already love Abbie Tucker, I would follow Madcap Betty Courtland to the ends of the world!"

"Gordon!" Dan's face contorted. "It wasn't delirium? She *was* actually here? She held me in her arms, told me —" He sank back as if too weak to go on. "That moment I knew I was crossing from life here to life eternal, did she kiss me?"

"That is only for her to say." Gordon stood. "A doctor sees many things that are sacred. He keeps them to himself. I only told you what I did to be fair to Betty." Gordon clasped Dan's hand. "Once you told me of your mother. 'Mrs. Minister,' I believe she was called. I think there's going to be another 'Mrs. Minister' right here in Pioneer as soon as you are able to attend a wedding." He cleared his throat and walked through the door, nearly falling over Betty, who was huddled behind the curtain. "Miss Courtland, I believe your patient wants to see you."

Betty hesitated. The moment she both hoped for and dreaded was here.

"Come here, Betty." The command in his dark eyes reached across the room and across the awkward moment that should have been between them.

"Oh, Daniel," she choked. She stumbled to his bed, dropped to her knees beside him, and buried her face in the coverlet.

"Look at me, Betty."

She forced herself to meet his compelling gaze.

"Why? Just to prove you could?"

She could not bear the sadness mingled with hope. "Because I love you." She cast pride aside as once she threw off discarded garments. "I have always loved you. If you died, my world would be ashes."

His hands cradled the tearstained face turned toward him. "You really mean it? You will actually live here in Pioneer with me, stand the hardships and do the work God has given me to do?"

"It's my work too."

Her fervent response sent flames leaping into the watching dark eyes. "You know God is still first." His steady gaze never left her own. "There can be no more choosing between you."

Betty's answer was firm. "I also know I am second only to the Lord Jesus, as you are to me. I have been called to serve even as you are called, but in a different way. Even if you had not lived, the Lord would still have been head of this household." She broke off, lips trembling. "But, oh, Daniel I am so glad He didn't take you away when I had just learned what it was to really care!"

"Betty." Two arms that would grow strong again and protect her from whatever life had to offer encircled her, drew her close. His lips claimed hers. Betty sighed, responding with all her heart. His love was everything she had dreamed of and more.

When he finally released her, her face was flushed, her eyes shone. In that moment Betty saw into his very soul and thanked God for the man he was. His whisper carried only to her listening ears.

"Mrs. Minister — welcome home."

The employees of Thorndike Press hope you have enjoyed this Large Print book. All our Large Print titles are designed for easy reading, and all our books are made to last. Other Thorndike Press Large Print books are available at your library, through selected bookstores, or directly from us.

For information about titles, please call:

(800) 223-1244
(800) 223-6121

To share your comments, please write:

Publisher
Thorndike Press
295 Kennedy Memorial Drive
Waterville, ME 04901